TOO LATE

(A Morgan Stark FBI Suspense Thriller—Book 1)

Rylie Dark

Rylie Dark

Bestselling author Rylie Dark is author of the SADIE PRICE FBI SUSPENSE THRILLER series, comprising six books (and counting); the MIA NORTH FBI SUSPENSE THRILLER series, comprising six books (and counting); the CARLY SEE FBI SUSPENSE THRILLER, comprising six books (and counting); and the MORGAN STARK FBI SUSPENSE THRILLER, comprising three books (and counting).

An avid reader and lifelong fan of the mystery and thriller genres, Rylie loves to hear from you, so please feel free to visit www.ryliedark.com to learn more and stay in touch.

ISBN: 978-1-0943-9509-8

BOOKS BY RYLIE DARK

SADIE PRICE FBI SUSPENSE THRILLER
ONLY MURDER (Book #1)
ONLY RAGE (Book #2)
ONLY HIS (Book #3)
ONLY ONCE (Book #4)
ONLY SPITE (Book #5)
ONLY MADNESS (Book #6)

MIA NORTH FBI SUSPENSE THRILLER
SEE HER RUN (Book #1)
SEE HER HIDE (Book #2)
SEE HER SCREAM (Book #3)
SEE HER VANISH (Book #4)
SEE HER GONE (Book #5)
SEE HER DEAD (Book #6)

CARLY SEE FBI SUSPENSE THRILLER
NO WAY OUT (Book #1)
NO WAY BACK (Book #2)
NO WAY HOME (Book #3)
NO WAY LEFT (Book #4)
NO WAY UP (Book #5)
NO WAY TO DIE (Book #6)

MORGAN STARK FBI SUSPENSE THRILLER
TOO LATE (Book #1)
TOO CLOSE (Book #2)
TOO FAR GONE (Book #3)

PROLOGUE

Michelle pulled her coat tighter around her neck as she left the hospital for the night and headed into the brisk D.C. fog. It had been a long shift—too long. She couldn't sustain work hours like this, and a talk with her boss was long overdue.

Maybe she shouldn't have switched hospitals. She now had the least amount of seniority of anyone in the department, and that meant she worked nights, weekends, and holidays. She'd taken for granted being able to pick and choose. She'd been dazzled by the promise of a signing bonus, along with an increase in pay.

Michelle tried to think of other things as she walked quickly down the street. The blue light of television sets flickered behind a few drawn curtains, but most of the windows were dark. Reasonable people with reasonable bosses had already gone to bed.

The images of the day kept flashing through her mind—the endless flow of patients, the suffering, the impatient doctors, the results she knew would be bad news to be delivered to patients—and she shook her head vigorously as if she could shake the thoughts free.

No more. She'd think about all that tomorrow.

She tried to think of happier things. Of the frozen meal awaiting her at home, of a night of comedy reruns, a glass of chardonnay big enough to swim in. Separating work from her life was getting to be a harder and harder endeavor.

The noise snapped her out of it.

She looked around quickly, her skin crawling at the sudden sound, and saw only an empty street behind her. Parked cars lined the narrow avenue, but she couldn't see anything else in the darkness and fog.

Too late. It was too late to be going home this time of night. She glanced at her watch—nearly 11. She chided herself. She had meant to leave at 7. Again.

Michelle increased her pace. Home was only a few blocks away now.

But then, it came again. The noise.

She stopped again. Michelle peered through the fog in the dim streetlight.

"Hello?" she called, her voice trembling. She was so close to home now. She didn't need this. It wasn't any of her business. She kept on walking, calmly and purposefully, as if she hadn't heard anything.

But she had.

The noise hadn't come from a car. It was too sharp. She heard it again. A sharp, short crack. It didn't sound like a gunshot, either. So what was it?

She walked faster.

It was coming from somewhere behind her. What if someone was hurt? What if they needed help? What if she switched on the news tomorrow and saw that someone she could have helped had died, right here, a few blocks from her apartment?

Michelle stopped in her tracks. She turned around.

The street seemed innocent in the light of the streetlamp. Peaceful in the silence. A little bit of fog clung to the lamppost, where it cast a web of shadows on the ground below.

She retraced her steps, her heart pounding in her chest as she proceeded.

Then it came again. The noise. Closer this time. To her left.

She stopped there, frozen, while the sound echoed against the buildings around her. A small alleyway opened off the street, snaking into the dark between two buildings. Dark and empty except for a shape huddled on the ground.

It didn't move. Probably just a pile of trash.

But what if someone was hurt?

Michelle walked quickly—almost ran—to the alley entrance, her breathing heavy. She could feel her heart pounding in her chest.

It wasn't a pile of trash. It was a man lying on the ground, clutching his head. His glasses had been knocked off and smashed, and his face was covered in blood.

He groaned, the noise cutting through the foggy silence.

She rushed over to him, her adrenaline kicking in, back in work mode.

"Are you OK?" she asked. "Can you breathe? Talk to me!"

She frantically checked his pulse.

It was weak, but there.

But there was so much blood.

She pulled out her phone, dialed 9-1-1.

"911. What is your emergency?"

“There's a man down here. He's hurt. He's bleeding. I think he's been mugged.” That must be it. She didn’t see any other reason for him to be in injured like this in the alley.

“Can you give me your location?”

Michelle stood and ran to the end of the alley to be sure she had the right cross streets. “I’m near the intersection of Roxboro Place and 8th Street Northwest.”

“I’ve got police and an ambulance on their way to you, ma’am. Do you want to stay on the line with me? Is there any chance you’re in danger?”

Michelle looked around. The street was deserted. Whoever had hurt this man was long gone. “No. I’m fine. I’ll wait for the emergency personnel.” She hung up and hurried back to the man.

“I've called 911. They'll be here soon. Just hold on.” Her voice shook.

His brown eyes stared up at her, pleading for help. He beckoned for her to come closer. She'd done what she could. She'd called the authorities. She listened hard for the sound of sirens.

The man's eyes continued to stare up at her, imploring her to do something to help.

Michelle had to do something, anything to relieve his pain even if it was only for a moment. She slipped off her coat and folded it, easing it under his head to use as a pillow. She shivered in the cold.

“What happened?” she asked. “Were you attacked? Mugged?”

She glanced around again. What if she was wrong? What if whoever had done this was still here? But there was no other movement in the alley and the only sound was the man's ragged breathing and the pounding of her own heart.

She looked a little closer to see if she could find the source of the blood on his face. In the dim light, she couldn't make out any cut or abrasion. She brushed his hair back from his forehead as much to comfort him as to look for his injury.

But then, suddenly, Michelle felt it. An icy cold hand on her wrist. A strong grip. Too strong.

He was squeezing her. Hurting her.

Sitting up. Smiling.

Her mind raced, trying to make it all make sense. Had he not actually been hurt? Had he been faking it?

He pulled out a knife.

“NO!” she cried out, trying to wrench her hand away from him. But she couldn't. His grasp was too strong. She started to panic.

“I wanted you to see me,” he said. “I wanted you to know who I am.”

She gasped and pulled harder at her hand.

“You should've kept walking,” he said.

He started to pull Michelle towards him by the arm, deeper into the shadows. She was fighting, but it was no use.

“Please,” she pleaded. “Just leave me alone. Take my purse. Whatever.”

He laughed. “I don't want your money.”

Who was this man? Why would he want her to know who he was? It made no sense. None of it made sense.

She tried to yell out. To scream. To warn someone. Anyone.

But he was on top of her. He was too strong.

She felt something hard, cold, and metallic against her throat.

She closed her eyes.

And then all was darkness.

CHAPTER ONE

Morgan Stark, MD, strode down the corridor toward the Neurology ward at Georgetown Hospital, white coat flapping behind him. He'd called the nurses' desk twice and gotten no reply.

Heads would roll about that. Later.

Right now, he needed to make sure no one took Vincenzo Rohr into surgery and apparently the only way to do that was to do it himself. Typical. "What do you know about fibromuscular dysplasia, Dr. Windham?"

"Fibro what?" Lexa Windham, his resident, had broken into a trot to keep up with him.

"Fibromuscular dysplasia," he repeated. It wasn't a fair question and he knew it. The disorder was rare, not something a resident would have seen this early in her rotation.

Most people didn't know about it even if they had it.

Vincenzo certainly didn't know. Nor had any of his other doctors figured it out, but it was almost certainly the cause of the aneurysm in his brain that was threatening to burst and of the two previous aneurysms he'd survived.

Morgan wasn't so sure that Vincenzo would survive this surgery if he was correct in his diagnosis. It was somewhat of a miracle that he'd survived the first two. Each subsequent insult to his body made the danger grow. The last thing they needed was for the third time to be the charm that killed him.

Lexa tapped the term into her phone while still keeping pace with Morgan. "Fibromuscular dysplasia is a genetic condition that can both enlarge and narrow the arteries causing weakness in arterial walls that can lead to aneurysms, stroke, or dissected arteries." Her steps faltered.

Morgan banged open the door to the stairs and held it for Lexa. He wasn't waiting for an elevator. "And what could that mean for Mr. Rohr?"

Lexa took the stairs two at a time, a sense of urgency hurrying her steps. "The added pressure on the arterial walls during a surgical procedure could cause multiple arteries to simply shred. They wouldn't be able to keep him from bleeding out right there on the table."

Good girl. She was quick, mentally and physically. With her dark hair pulled back into a low ponytail and her bright blue eyes, she reminded him of Fiona. Fiona had been on her way to being a star resident, too. How many lives might his little sister have saved if she'd been able to go forward?

There was no time to reminisce or speculate now, though, about what might have been. Morgan hurried to keep up with Lexa's quick ascension of the stairs, their foot strikes echoing on the concrete.

"You told them they shouldn't open him up," Lexa said, hitting the top of the stairs and hurrying into the corridor. "Not until you had some time to go over his files."

"I did," Morgan agreed. "So, let's make sure they don't."

"So what are you thinking?" she panted with exertion. "Without the surgery, that aneurysm is likely to rupture. Then there's risk of stroke and brain damage."

"I'm thinking an angiogram. That will show us how the blood is flowing so we can find the weak spots." The contrast dye they'd inject into Rohr would light up and they could see places where his arteries were already leaking. Morgan stopped at the unattended nurse's desk and cursed. Where was everyone?

He glanced up at the board. Vincenzo was in Room 32C. Just around the corner. He took off again, Lexa at his heels. Together, they burst into the room.

It was empty.

Where the hell was Vincenzo Rohr?

Was he too late?

What had been a bright, sunny morning had turned into a dark and gloomy afternoon. Rain lashed at the windows, making the empty hospital room feel almost sub-aquatic. The rain drumming on the roof sounded like loud, cheap bamboo sticks.

Morgan turned in a circle as if his patient might suddenly appear from one of the corners. A dark-haired, dark-skinned nurse wearing maroon scrubs came into the room with an armful of linens. "Dr. Stark," she said, brown eyes going a little wide. Her name tag read Isabella.

"Where's my patient, Isabella?" There was no time to waste with pleasantries.

"Dr. Ayres took him to surgery. He said they couldn't wait any longer. They needed to deal with the aneurysm before it burst." Isabella set the linens down and took a step backward.

Morgan shut his eyes for a moment, trying to contain his rage. Damn Ayres, freaking scalpel jockey. “Which room?”

Isabella's mouth gaped a little farther open and she twisted her hands together in front of herself. “I d-d-on't understand. Which room what?”

“Which operating room? Where is my patient?” He knew it wasn't this young woman's fault, but damn it, a man's life hung in the balance.

“Three,” Isabella blurted out. “What should I—?”

Morgan didn't hear the rest of her words because he was already running down the hall, his heart pounding in his ears and Lexa right behind him. Down the hall with its yellow linoleum tile and buzzing fluorescent lights, Morgan thundered, a bull searching for the red cape.

He waved his ID badge over the RFID reader and the double doors into the operating room suites clicked and swung forward in a slow arc. He shoved them aside. He had to get into that room before Ayres sunk a knife into Rohr and set off a reaction they wouldn't be able to stop.

Morgan flung open the door to OR Three's anteroom. One of the scrub nurses was still by the sinks. “Hey,” the man called. “You can't go in there.”

Ignoring him, Morgan grabbed a surgical mask off a pile by the door and covered his face as he shoved open the doors. Behind him, he heard Lexa running interference for him with the scrub nurse. “Trust me, Ayres is going to want to hear what Dr. Stark has to say,” she said.

“You sure about that?” the man said.

Morgan almost snorted. That was a scrub nurse who knew his surgeon. Ayres rarely wanted to hear want anyone had to say except himself.

Morgan rushed to the table, relieved to see that Vincenzo was under, but the procedure hadn’t yet started, although Ayres had a scalpel in his hand and was getting ready to make the first cut, clearly intending to clip the aneurysm in an open craniotomy. Thank heavens. He’d made it in time.

“Stop!” Morgan yelled. “You cut him, you kill him.”

CHAPTER TWO

Ayres whirled around. "What the hell are you doing in my OR, Stark?"

Morgan skidded to a stop. Ayres wasn't a big man, but he carried himself like he was. Plus, he held a very sharp scalpel in his hand. "Trying to save your patient, Jason." Maybe a personal plea would help his case.

Ayres's eyes narrowed at him over his mask. "Explain yourself."

His tone was imperious. It made Morgan grind his teeth. He got it. Really, he did. Surgeons have to be cocky. They have to have courage of their convictions. They make a lot of tough calls and everything they do carries a certain amount of risk.

He didn't have to like them, though, and he often didn't. He took a deep breath and blew it out, willing himself to remain calm. For a few seconds, the only sound in the room was the beeping of the monitors tracking Vincenzo's heart and respiration.

The scrub nurse had made it around Lexa. "I'm sorry, Dr. Ayres. He got past me."

Ayres held up the hand that wasn't holding the scalpel. "It's okay, Malik. Let's hear what Dr. Stark has to say for himself." He turned back toward Morgan. "Well?"

"Vincenzo Rohr has a relatively rare genetic disorder. Fibromuscular dysplasia. It's likely what caused the aneurysm and the ones before it." Morgan finished tying the surgical mask around his face with practiced fingers and walked a few more steps toward the table where Vincenzo lay motionless.

Shaking his head before Morgan could get any closer, Ayres said, "No. That doesn't make any sense. He's had two prior successful aneurysm clippings. If he had fibromuscular dysplasia he would have bled out during one of those."

"Not necessarily," Morgan took another step in. He'd pull the damn scalpel out of Ayres's hand if he had to. "With each subsequent insult to those arterial walls, his chances of a good outcome go down. He's been lucky so far, but there's no guarantee he'll be lucky a third time. Look at the numbers. The time between his second and third aneurysms is about half the time between the first and the second. His condition is getting worse. The arterial walls are getting weaker."

Ayres lowered the hand that held the scalpel with an irritating slowness. "How sure are you about this? Because I'm pretty sure that aneurysm is going to blow soon."

"I'm very sure." Morgan glanced over his shoulder to check on Lexa. Her ponytail was a little askew, but she seemed otherwise unharmed by her skirmish with Malik even if he was easily four inches taller and forty pounds heavier. "Sure enough that I was going to let my resident tackle your scrub nurse so I could get in here to stop you from doing this procedure."

The anesthesiologist snorted. Ayres threw her a look and the woman turned her attention to her instruments. Ayres never had much of a sense of humor. He put the scalpel back on the tray, though. That was all Morgan really wanted, to get that knife away from Vincenzo's head so there was a chance he could watch his two-year-old daughter grow up.

Ayres gestured at his team. "Get Rohr into recovery." Then he turned back to Morgan. "Let's go figure out how to save this man's life, then."

"I've got some ideas about that," Morgan said, tensing as he waited to see how cooperative Ayres was going to be.

Ayres snorted and waved for Morgan to follow him out of the room. "Why am I not surprised to hear that? Let's hear it."

"We put him on beta blockers to lessen the pressure on those arterial walls and then we do an angiogram. We'll be able to keep an eye on any place a leak is even threatening and pull back if necessary. If we work together on it, we can be in and out before we do any more harm. Then we can get Vincenzo over to vascular services and let them take over long term treatment of his condition." It took Morgan a second to realize they were heading into the waiting room.

The second they walked in, a young woman sitting on the couch stood up. She was a sweet-faced woman in her late twenties who had nearly been enveloped by the threadbare sprung sofa in the waiting room. "The surgery is done already?" She looked up at the clock on the waiting room wall and then back at Ayres.

"No. We're going to postpone the surgery for at least another day or two. Dr. Stark here will explain why." Ayres gestured at Morgan.

Morgan dragged a straight back chair from the corner closer to where Rohr's wife stood. He sat and motioned for her to sit back down as well. "Ms. Rohr," he began.

"Sofia, please." she interrupted.

"Sofia, then. Your husband has a rare condition called fibromuscular dysplasia. It causes a weakening of the arterial walls."

Sofia frowned.

He cast about in his mind for a way to simplify the explanation. "It's why Vincenzo is developing these aneurysms. We need to be extra careful in how we fix this aneurysm and then we can treat Vincenzo for the underlying condition so he doesn't get another one."

Sofia looked up at Morgan, big brown eyes both hopeful and worried. "So Vincenzo will be all right?" The couple's daughter sat at her feet, stacking blocks on the coffee table.

Ayres cut in before Morgan could answer. He'd been standing near the doorway, checking his phone while Morgan explained Vincenzo's diagnosis and how they planned to go forward. "We think so. Vincenzo is stable for the moment. We'll start him on beta blockers. We should be able to go in with an angiogram to fix the aneurysm once all the dust settles. Meanwhile, we've sent him for a CTA to confirm the diagnosis."

Typical surgeon. Obviously he was going to try to take credit for the save. Let him. Morgan couldn't care less about who got the credit for it. All he cared about was that the save actually happened. Then Ayres surprised Morgan by saying, "We wouldn't have known without Dr. Stark here. It's possible that Vincenzo would have been okay through this surgery as he was with the previous two, but there's no guarantee he would have had a good outcome."

Morgan might have to rethink his opinion of surgeons. At least, of this one.

Sofia silently mouthed the words good outcome. Morgan saw the moment when Ayres's meaning dawned on her. He wasn't a huge fan of euphemisms, preferring straight talk. Sometimes a softer touch was a good idea, though. Sofia's lower lip trembled a little, then she said, "Thank you, Dr. Stark. Thank you so much. You, too, Dr. Ayres. And – " Looking a little confused she glanced at Lexa.

Lexa smiled. She really was the spitting image of Fiona. Even that little tic she had of straightening her ponytail when she was working up her courage was something Morgan remembered Fiona doing. "I'm Dr. Windham. I'm a resident working with Dr. Stark."

Morgan's cell phone buzzed. He pulled it out of his pocket and glanced at the Caller ID, swiped the button to send it to voicemail, and turned back to Sofia. Now was not the time to take a call from his soon-to-be ex-wife.

He stood up, getting ready to leave, but Lexa gave a little head nod toward the little girl. Oh, right. The other part of the news to deliver. He sat back down. “Sofia, there’s one more thing that’s important to mention. Fibromuscular dysplasia is a genetic disorder. Do you understand what that means?”

Sofia nodded. “Yes. It means it’s passed down through the family.”

“It would probably be a good idea to get your daughter tested as well.” Morgan glanced over at Lexa. “Dr. Windham can help you get that set up.”

By the look on Sofia’s face, she hadn’t put that together yet. He felt like a heel, but better they should know what they were dealing with. Maybe they could avoid the little girl having some of the issues her father had.

They said their good-byes and Ayres and Morgan walked to the doctors’ lounge. Outside the door, Ayres stopped. “I’ve got to get to my next procedure. I wanted to thank you, though. It’s a pleasure working with you.” He stuck out his hand.

Morgan took it, but didn’t comment.

His lack of enthusiasm was not wasted on Ayres. “I mean it, Morgan. Yes. I was pissed as hell when you disrupted my OR, but you saved my patient. Our patient. Sure. Maybe it would have been okay. Maybe Vincenzo would have come through one more procedure. But maybe he wouldn’t have. Then that little girl back there would be growing up without her Daddy.” Ayres’s eyes clouded up for a second and he coughed. “You and I both know that there are some patients who can’t be saved, but Vincenzo isn’t one of them. I would not have wanted that on my conscience for the rest of my life.”

He turned and walked down the hall, back toward the Neurology Department.

Morgan watched him go, trying to get a handle on all the feelings surging through him. That had definitely taken a turn he hadn’t expected. Maybe Ayres wasn’t quite the scalpel jockey Morgan had thought he was. He went into the lounge to wait for Lexa. His cell phone buzzed again, this time with an incoming text. He sighed. Ashley asking him to call when he had a minute to talk. So civil. So polite. So utterly depressing.

Sometimes he wished she'd scream at him, throw stuff against the wall. It would be easier to handle than the sadness he saw in those big blue eyes of hers.

He did everything he could think of to make the doctors' lounge coffee drinkable, adding enough cream and sugar so that the damn thing might as well be a milkshake. Still, it tasted nothing but bitter.

Maybe it wasn't the coffee's fault. Maybe that bad taste was permanently in his own mouth.

He sat down at the long table, scarred with water marks, and leaned back looking at the ceiling, long legs extended in front of him. Fatigue dragged at him. There was a time that the coffee wouldn't have mattered. It could have been made from actual horse dung and still would have tasted sweet.

He'd loved his job and a save like this one would have made him feel like he was flying. That family would stay intact. He could see the tangible results of his hard work and study.

Why wasn't it enough anymore?

He looked down at his phone again. Did it have to do with Ashley?

Maybe.

While he'd poured his attention and focus on other people's lives and families, he'd neglected his own and now he was losing that. Ash wanted a divorce.

If he didn't have his marriage and his job no longer kept him going, what was the point? He didn't know.

The room was like so much else in the hospital. Generic. Unremarkable. Two couches and a coffee table with nearly every major medical journal in the country strewn across it, clogged with the stench of old coffee and the lingering scent of burned coffee grounds.

Yet, some of the finest doctors in the United States regularly sat in this room, humbled as Morgan was now, by the mysteries of the human bodies they tried so hard to save. Humbled by the hubris it took to think that they could change people's fates.

Morgan sat up at the sound of the door creaking open. His green scrubs pulled at his broad shoulders and he shrugged against them. "How'd it go?" His voice came out in a croak.

"Good. Or as good as it could be." Lexa went to the counter to get herself a cup of coffee. "No one wants to hear that their child might have a genetic disorder that will follow her for the rest of her life. Still, if the daughter has the condition, you probably just saved her life as well as her father's."

She sat down across from Morgan, turning the coffee cup around in slow circles in front of her. “How did you know to look for fibromuscular dysplasia? What clued you in?”

Morgan rubbed the back of his neck. “It was the combination of symptoms. The aneurysms for sure. Add in the tinnitus, the occasional blood pressure spikes, and the migraines, and it all came together.”

“For you.” She took a sip of her coffee and made a face. Maybe the bitterness wasn’t all in Morgan’s head, after all. “It didn't come together for anyone else. I was thinking maybe Ehlers-Danlos or even Loeys-Dietz.”

“That’s great, Lexa. You were on the right track. You’d have figured out that it was something genetic. You were only one step away.” Every time Morgan looked at Lexa, he saw Fiona. Lexa was about the same age as Fiona was when she'd disappeared. The coloring was there with the dark hair and blue eyes. There was more to it, though. There was an inquisitiveness, a curiosity coupled with a first-class mind.

As much as Morgan enjoyed having his resident acknowledge his expertise, he would have much rather had his little sister there next to him. Man, the team they would have made.

“A step that would have been too late if Ayres had cracked his skull. Me almost diagnosing Rohr correctly after he died on the table wouldn’t have given Sofia back her husband or given Catalina back her father.” She bowed her head. Her dark hair glinted in the harsh fluorescent light.

Poor kid. She was way too hard on herself. She was right, though. People’s lives were in their hands. “So what kept you from making that one last step?” he asked.

Lexa looked up at him. “I thought I should look at environmental factors, too. Maybe he’d been exposed to something at work or at home that could have triggered the aneurysms.”

“But your first instinct was that it was genetic?” Morgan leaned forward, elbows on the table supporting him. She’d been so close. What had stopped her? What had she let get in her way? “Why not pursue that fully before switching to a different avenue of thought?”

Lexa sighed. “I was worried I was wasting my time looking at genetic possibilities and thought I should hedge my bets.”

Ah. Morgan got the picture. “There is no bet hedging in this business. It’s literally life and death every day. You have to have the courage of your convictions. You have to learn to trust yourself.”

“I . . . I’m just not sure how to do that. There’s so much I still don’t know,” Lexa said.

“And that’s why you’re a resident working under an attending physician. Most residents wouldn’t have made it anywhere near as far as you did. I know. I’ve trained more than a few.” He knew he had a knack for figuring out the tricky diagnoses, the ones with multiple factors. He suspected that Lexa would, too. She had that kind of brain. She just needed a bit more time, a little more experience under her belt. She’d get there and it would be a pleasure watching her grow and develop. Working with her had brought back some of the delight he’d always taken in his work that he’d found hard to reach lately. “You should go home. Get some sleep. After, of course, you schedule me in for that angiogram on Vincenzo.”

Lexa frowned at him. “You're going to do it yourself?”

“Best way I know of to make sure it's done right.” The only way to make sure it was done right. His opinion of Ayres might have risen some, but not that far yet.

Lexa pushed back her chair. “You'll be going home soon, then, too?”

He nodded. “Of course.”

He smiled at Lexa, not wanting her to know that the thought of returning to his apartment, and what he had to do when he got there tonight, filled him with a sense of dread.

CHAPTER THREE

Morgan got off the elevator on the fifth floor and stared down the hallway of his apartment building. No wonder he spent so much time at the hospital. Blank walls marred only by the occasional scrape from someone's bicycle as they'd wheeled it out of the building. Blank doors on each side. No windows. No skylights. No personality. It was a place for people who were passing through, the only marks they made accidental, anonymous.

Home should be a refuge, a place to replenish and reenergize. His characterless generic apartment was anything but that. It was one more thing that drained him, that sucked the marrow right out of his bones. Night after night, he convinced himself that it was temporary, but he was pretty certain that tonight's conversation with Ashley would put an end to that delusion.

No. This was his life now and he wasn't sure he wanted to face it.

He'd had some hopes that he'd only be passing through here in this furnished apartment when he'd moved in a year ago. Look how that had turned out.

He unlocked the door and dumped his bag and coat and the take-out dinner he'd picked up on the kitchen counter. The cleaning service had been there. Everything was clean, tidy, and oh, so very impersonal. He missed tripping over the shoes that Ashley used to kick off by the door of their house in Alexandria and having to shove aside the jumble of whatever craft project she'd embarked on to get to the dinner table. He hadn't realized what a privilege it was to make room for someone in his life, to share in their joys and sorrows, to laugh with them and, yes, to cry with them, too.

He should have done a better job of it.

He pulled a beer out of the fridge, popped the cap off the bottle, and took a long pull of it, grimacing a little at the hoppy aftertaste. Without sitting down, he pulled a fork out of a drawer and ate a few bites of the chicken vindaloo he'd picked up at the corner Indian place. It was already cold. Sighing, he put the fork down.

He really couldn't put it off any longer. He pulled out his phone and hit the button to place the call he'd been dreading.

"Hey, thanks for calling me back." It didn't matter how long it had been since Ashley left Louisiana. There was always a honeyed hint of the south in her accent. It still made his heart beat a little faster.

"Of course." He heard the little catch in her breath and knew what it meant. If he'd been a little better at things like returning her calls, he might not be living in a furnished apartment in downtown D.C. He might still be out in Alexandria with her. "I don't suppose this has to do with hospital business." Ashley was an Assistant Director of Administration at Georgetown.

"No. It's about us. Did you get the papers I sent?"

He sat down in the recliner chair across from the television set and pushed back. "I did."

"And?"

"And I'll get them signed this week. They have to be notarized and I haven't had the time to figure out where to do that." He'd been a little busy trying to figure out Vincenzo Rohr's diagnosis and keeping another doctor from inadvertently killing the man.

"Want me to research that for you?"

That was Ashley all over. Always looking for those little ways to help, to make his life easier. He hadn't fully realized all she did until she wasn't there to do it anymore.

"No. I'll figure it out."

"Thanks. Please do, Morgan. I think it's time for us to wrap this up."

"Is it?" He cringed at the pleading note in his voice. "Are you sure, Ash?"

She made another little noise that he recognized all too well. She was crying. "I wish I wasn't, Morgan. I really do." She didn't sound so sure. So why was she pushing it?

"Is there someone else?"

There was a pause and he braced for the news he didn't want to hear. Then she said, "No, Morgan. There's not anyone else."

He blew out a breath with relief. It wasn't like she wasn't entitled to start dating. He just didn't want to think about it, to imagine some other man's hands on her, to picture another man's lips against that sensitive spot on her neck.

"The problem is that there's always someone else for you," she said, sounding firmer. "Your patients."

It wasn't that she'd never come first with him. She thought that, but she was wrong. It was that he himself had never come first. His relationships, his needs were always secondary – sometimes tertiary – to his patients' needs. He'd needed her, but that had to come last.

"Did you just get home?" she asked.

"Yeah. A few minutes ago." He wasn't sure what she was getting at.

"Do you know what time it is?"

He glanced up at the clock on the wall. Nearly nine o'clock. Now he got it. He'd stayed way later at the hospital than he'd intended. As he had on way too many nights when he and Ashley had been together. "I . . . I could change."

She laughed. "Tell me one thing you did today that you would have been able to walk away from to come home earlier and it can't be eating, drinking, or going to the bathroom."

He cast his mind back over the day's events. Figuring out Vincenzo's diagnosis. Trying to reach the nurses' station. Going there himself. Interrupting the surgery. Collaborating with Ayres to figure out how to go forward. Talking to the patient's wife. All the paperwork that had to be kept up on so that insurance companies and hospital administration would okay everything.

"There isn't anything, is there?" she asked, her voice gone soft.

She knew him too well. "It was an emergency."

"It was always an emergency." She answered so quickly that she must have known what he was going to say before he even knew himself. "Get the papers signed, Morgan."

"I will. I'm sorry, Ash."

"I know."

She hung up.

Morgan stayed there for a while, staring at the ceiling, the beer suspended by its long neck between two fingers. He should get up and go to bed. It had been a long ass day and tomorrow wouldn't be any shorter. He thought about texting Lexa to find out what time she'd scheduled Rohr's angiogram for, but then thought better of it. He clicked the television on instead.

Let Lexa have her evening. In fact, he should be sure to have her leave the hospital earlier. Make sure she went home, had some time for a social life, for her family. Hell. Maybe she should even have a hobby.

The last thing he wanted for Lexa was to end up thirty-five years old, alone, staring at the popcorn ceiling of a crappy apartment with nothing but a beer and a television set for company. She was too special to have her life not come to more than that.

He drained the rest of his beer and headed into the kitchen to pour himself something stronger. Behind him, the news anchor finished bantering with his co-anchor, his voice going suddenly plummy and serious. “A twenty-five-year-old Brentwood woman, a laboratory technician at Bridgepoint Hospital, was found dead on the street near her home last night . . .”

CHAPTER FOUR

Lexa put her head down and pushed into the wind. The storm that had turned Vincenzo Rohr's hospital room into a gloomy cave earlier in the day had passed, but the wind still whipped at the trees and the air held a damp chill. When would spring start?

The apartment she shared with two other residents was in a building only a few blocks from the Metro. Washington was one of those cities where owning a car could be more of a hindrance than a help. Traffic was nearly always snarled, parking was expensive, and the Metro was clean and safe and convenient if you planned your life well. Lexa was nothing if not a planner. Still, these few blocks at this time of night and in this weather compounded the weariness that was an everyday reality for residents.

She distracted herself from her discomfort by going over the day's events in her head. Fibromuscular dysplasia. Morgan's diagnosis wasn't just brilliant. It had also been arrived at fast enough for him to save Vincenzo's life. Lexa's heart clutched a little thinking about Rohr's little daughter, carefully stacking her blocks in the waiting room, unaware of the drama around her. If it had been left to Lexa, Catalina would have never gotten to really know her father. She might not even remember him.

She'd been so close, too! Only a few steps behind the great Morgan Stark. A few steps behind was still behind, though. If only she'd kept looking at those genetic possibilities and not distracted herself with possible environmental causes. She wanted to kick herself. Why hadn't she listened to her gut? Morgan was right. She needed to have the courage of her convictions. She made a little vow to trust herself more. After all, how were patients supposed to trust her if she didn't trust herself?

The door to her apartment building finally appeared in view. She let herself into the lobby and took a second to appreciate being out of the wind. The lobby seemed almost eerily quiet after the noise of the wind in the trees outside. Warmth began to seep back into her cold toes and fingers and she unzipped her jacket. After stopping at the mailboxes, she went around the corner to get the elevator to her fourth-floor apartment only to be greeted by a piece of paper taped to the doors. Out of order.

Crap. She leaned her forehead against the closed doors. She was so tired. All she wanted to do was get to her bed and collapse for a few hours. For a second, she contemplated sitting down in the corner of the lobby and going to sleep there. She was that tired. Then she thought about Catalina Rohr, how the work she'd been part of at the hospital that day had made it possible for that little girl to have a father. She was a doctor, God damn it. Yes. It was hard, but it was so worth it.

Lexa pulled herself up straight. Four stupid flights of stairs weren't going to stop her. They were one more thing for her to conquer. She flung open the door to the stairs and marched up.

The stairwell was nearly as cold as it was outside. The smell of damp concrete and something else odd and metallic tickled Lexa's nose. The iron railing was cold under her hand and the peeling paint on it scratched a bit as she ascended. Hitting the landing for the first floor, she paused to catch her breath. The smell was stronger here. What was it? It was familiar, but she couldn't quite place it. Not her problem. She shook her head and started up the next flight.

She was halfway up the next flight when she saw the shoe. It took her a second to make sense of it. She was that tired. For a moment, it seemed like it was hanging in mid-air. Then she realized it was on a foot that was attached to a leg that had to belong to someone who was lying face down on the next landing.

Fatigue forgotten, she raced up the next stairs. She'd been right. A man lay face down on the scuffed concrete, a pool of blood spreading beneath him. That had been the metallic smell she'd noticed. Blood. Familiar, yet too out of place here in the stairwell for her to identify it.

Quickly, she knelt. She'd dealt with plenty of emergencies in the hospital, but there she had back up. Nurses and techs and other doctors. Plus all the equipment she could ever want or need. She was on her own here. She checked vitals, pressing her shaking fingers against his carotid. Okay good. A strong steady beat. He wasn't dead. Her own pounding heart slowed a little. Next she checked his neck. No fracture there, thank goodness.

So where was the blood coming from? She had to do something before he lost much more. That could be catastrophic.

She touched his shoulder. "Sir? Can you talk? Can you tell me what happened?"

He groaned in response.

Still unconscious. Okay. She wanted to get a sense of how severe the man's injuries were. She rolled him gently toward his side to assess what was going on. Blood covered the man's face. That explained it. He must have hit his head on the steps. Head wounds bled like crazy. He might not be too badly injured. It might look significantly worse than it actually was.

The man's eyes flew open, startlingly white in his blood-smeared face. He rolled the rest of the way over and grabbed her wrist with his left hand. She tried to pull loose, but his grip was unexpectedly strong. Then he sat up in one fluid motion and slashed at her with a knife he'd been holding hidden beneath him in his right hand. She felt nothing for a second and then a stinging sensation across her abdomen told her she'd been cut. She looked down to see blood soaking through her shirt.

"What the hell?" Lexa reared back and tried to stand at the same time. Her right foot hit the top stair at an angle and her ankle rolled. She windmilled her arms, trying to maintain her balance, but it was no good. In the next second, she toppled down the stairs, hitting concrete edges with her shoulder and hips. She wrapped her arms around her head, trying to protect it from the punishing steps.

Finally, she hit the landing below. A quick mental inventory told her she was banged up and bruised, but still okay. At the top of the landing, the man stared down at her, head cocked to one side as if evaluating the situation. The blood looked like a mask on his face. As she tried again to stand, he started toward her.

Who the hell was this guy? And why was he coming after her?

There was no time to consider the possibilities. She lurched to her feet, her ankle feeling unstable beneath her. There was no time to worry about what kind of damage she might be doing to her ligaments by running on an injured foot. She staggered down the next few steps.

"Help!" she screamed. "Someone help!"

Her voice echoed back to her, bouncing off the concrete around her. No one would hear her.

She pulled her phone from her jacket pocket, fumbling at the buttons as she tried to run. The man's footsteps were right behind her. She didn't dare to look back.

The metal door to the first-floor apartments came into view. If she could get through there, maybe someone would hear her. She heard the sound of a ringing coming through the speaker of her phone. Maybe she'd managed to connect with 911 somehow.

Another few steps and she'd be through the door. She reached for the knob, her fingers grasping it and then slipping off as someone grabbed her by her ponytail and pulled her back.

She screamed again as her neck arched backward and the man's blood-smeared face loomed into view.

CHAPTER FIVE

Morgan glanced at the clock. He'd been home for more than an hour. The Scotch in his glass was gone. He should really go to bed. The idea of the empty cold expanse of his mattress repelled him.

All those late nights through medical school and his residency when he'd slipped into a bed warmed by Ashley's body, lulled into sleep by her deep even breathing. He'd taken them for granted, assumed they would always be there.

He reached for his phone. Maybe he could convince Ashley that he would appreciate what he had this time around, that he'd make her his priority. Hell, he'd make himself a priority. His thumb hovered over the redial button. Her question from earlier in the evening running through his head. What would he have done differently? The answer was still nothing. He let the phone drop.

"I'm an idiot," he said to the empty room.

His phone buzzed as if to reply. He looked at the display. Lexa.

What was she calling about at this hour? He really would have to force her to have more of a life than he did.

He swiped to accept the call. "What's up, Lexa?"

Nothing. Well, not nothing. There were noises. Muffled and distant, but still noises. Probably a pocket dial.

"Lexa," he called a little louder, hoping to get her attention.

He turned up the volume, trying to figure out where she was and what was going on. Were those footsteps? Panting? Was she running somewhere?

Then her scream echoed through the phone.

"Lexa!" he called, louder this time. "Are you okay? Lexa, answer me!"

All he got for an answer was something that sounded like a whimper of pain. Then the call disconnected.

Before he even realized he'd made a decision, he was up and running for the door, keys in hand.

He thundered down the stairs, not willing to wait for the elevator, and out into the chilly night air. He ran for his car, entering Lexa's address into his GPS as he went.

He raced through the dark streets, grateful that it was late enough for the traffic that usually clogged the roads of D.C. to have dissipated. Was he overreacting? Should he call 911? He wasn't sure. All he could think was that he had to get to Lexa. Dodging into oncoming traffic, he zipped around the one car creeping along the street, its driver probably looking for parking. Ahead, a light turned yellow and he floored the accelerator, whooshing through the intersection. Horns blared behind him.

He didn't care.

All he could think of was Lexa. Lexa lying somewhere. Lexa in pain. He had to get to her. He could not lose her. He didn't think his heart could take another loss.

He took the next corner fast enough to feel like only two wheels were on the ground, but he'd made it there. Lexa's building. He left his car double-parked on the street and ran into the building.

"Lexa!" he called.

No one answered. He knew her apartment was on the fourth floor. He ran for the stairs, pushing the heavy door open and froze.

He knew what drying blood looked like and there was a long smear of it along the bare concrete of the stairs. The smell of it clogged the back of his throat. He looked up and saw that it streaked the stairs. Something – someone – who had been bleeding heavily had been dragged along here. He looked to see where the smear led and saw an exit door.

He shoved through it.

The cold air gusted, bringing a fine spray of grit up from the alleyway. Morgan squinted his eyes against it. The blood smear was fainter here, harder to make out, but still visible. Letting the door drop behind him, he was plunged into darkness. He pulled out his phone and launched the flashlight app, the harsh light throwing the stain into stark relief.

He followed it through the alley, still calling Lexa's name, but getting no answer. The trail he followed stopped abruptly. He turned in a circle, trying to figure out where to look next.

His heart nearly stopped when he saw the slender hand, so pale it nearly glowed, extending out from behind the Dumpster. He ran, skidding to his knees next to Lexa's unconscious body.

The blood had pooled beneath her. He ripped open her jacket to find the source and recoiled. It was everywhere. Whoever had done this had been in a frenzy. He couldn't even begin to count the stab wounds and he wasn't sure what to treat first. There were too many wounds, too much blood, too much damage. This couldn't be happening. Who would have done something like this? It was unreal. His mind couldn't seem to process it and for a second it wasn't Lexa he hovered over, but Fiona. He couldn't seem to get a full breath into his lungs. Panic swamped him and his vision blurred.

He shook his head hard. He had to snap out of it. He had to go into doctor mode. He needed to step back, to have that layer of distance between himself and his patient. Now when he looked, he saw Lexa, but her wounds were still devastating. Praying he wasn't too late, he dialed 911.

"911. What's your emergency?"

Despite the panic he felt, he called on his years of training to stay calm in the face of disaster. "This is Dr. Morgan Stark of Georgetown University Hospital. I am behind the apartment building at 237 Tompkins Avenue. There is a woman here who is bleeding heavily from multiple stab wounds. She is unconscious. I need an ambulance STAT!"

The sound of a computer keyboard being typed on came through the speaker of the phone. "Yes, Dr. Stark. I've got your location. Emergency personnel are on their way to you now."

"Good." He dropped the phone to the ground, leaving the connection open. "Lexa! Lexa, can you hear me?"

No response. He ripped off his shirt and wadded it up against her chest and abdomen, trying to stop the flow of blood from the wounds. The cold bit at him. He didn't care.

He pressed his fingers against her carotid. Dear God. No pulse. Quickly, he checked her airway. There was nothing blocking her mouth or throat. He tilted her head back and blew in two quick breaths, gratified to see her chest rise and fall. He checked her carotid again. Still nothing.

"I'm starting chest compressions," he barked to the phone.

Placing the heel of his hand in the center of her chest, he put his other hand on top of it and enlaced his fingers. He pushed in, praying he wasn't breaking any of her ribs.

"Come on, Lexa," he gasped out as he kept up the compressions at around two per second. He didn't know what else to do, what else to say. The need to save her was so strong in him that it threatened to overwhelm him. "Come on back."

He stopped and checked her carotid again. Still nothing. No no no. He blew in two rescue breaths. Her face was pale, so pale. He returned to the compressions again. Sirens wailed nearby and he prayed they were coming to him.

"Please, Lexa. Please come back."

Footsteps rang out in the alley behind him.

"Sir! We've got this." Strong hands pulled at his shoulders.

He kept going. How could he trust anyone else to do this? It had to be done right. It had to be done by him.

"Sir! Let us in there to help. Please!"

Two sets of hands interlaced his arms and pulled him back. He looked to either side. Police officers. The EMTs rushed in and took over, checking vitals and starting an IV line.

"She's a healthy twenty-five-year old woman," Morgan called to them. "No underlying conditions."

One of the EMTs glanced over her shoulder. "Get him out of here."

The officers dragged him backward away from Lexa. Panic seized him. "No!" he screamed. "I need to stay here. I need to be with her."

Morgan struggled against the arms holding him only to have them tighten. Damn it. He had to get back to Lexa. He had to get away from them. In desperation, he threw an elbow back and heard the officer grunt as Morgan connected with the man's solar plexus. He tried to slip free from the other officer's grasp only to have that grip tighten further.

Then suddenly Morgan was face down on the scarred cement of the alley floor. "That's it, buddy. You're coming downtown."

CHAPTER SIX

Morgan laid his head down on his pillowed arms, the metal table cold against his cheek. He had no idea how long he'd been in this gray, claustrophobic room at the police station. It could have been five minutes or five hours. At least he wasn't handcuffed anymore.

The cops had brought him here to this room and, after getting him a sweatshirt, the questions had started. Who was he? Who was Lexa to him? Why had he been in the alley? When had Lexa called him? What had she said? He'd answered everything multiple times. Then two more cops, these ones in suits rather than uniforms, circled around and asked the same things again in different ways, trying to catch him in a lie or an inconsistency. Morgan knew the technique. He used it on patients sometimes when he could tell they weren't giving him the whole truth. Come at the same thing from multiple angles and eventually you got a fuller picture.

The problem was that there was no fuller picture to get from Morgan. He'd told them everything he could think of. He wasn't holding anything back. He was willing to do anything he could do to help them catch the bastard who had done that to Lexa.

Lexa. Please, God, let Lexa be okay. It was a longshot. He knew all too well what all that blood had meant. Her face had been so pale, her gaze fixed. Maybe, though, maybe a miracle would happen and they'd be able to stitch her up and pump some blood into her. Maybe they could save her.

Damn it. He wanted to be at the hospital helping. He wanted to do something besides sit in this God forsaken interview room waiting for . . . what?

He was alone now. The two plainclothes cops had taken his phone to corroborate all that he'd told them about Lexa's call. Morgan had no idea how long they'd been gone. Time was losing its meaning. The room stank of stale coffee and sweat. The fluorescent light glared off the table, making Morgan's eyes sting. He shut them. One of the many handy skills he'd picked up as a resident was the ability to sleep almost anywhere at any time. He slowed his breathing and let his muscles relax. The sweet oblivion of unconsciousness softened the edges of his world.

The creak of the metal door opening had Morgan bolting upright. He checked his cheek quickly for drool and then looked at the woman who had walked in. She was tall, leggy. Long black hair pulled into a sleek low ponytail. She wore black slacks with a matching black blazer over a turquoise blouse. The blazer didn't hide the badge clipped to her belt or the firearm she carried.

She gave him a smile, notable in its lack of warmth, and said, "Dr. Stark, I am Special Agent Danielle Hernandez with the FBI. I'd like to ask you some questions." She had a slight accent, a tiny bit of sibilance.

The FBI? He stared at her, trying to get this all to make sense.

Without waiting for a response, she pulled out the chair across from him and sat. She extracted a yellow legal pad from her briefcase and a pen that she clicked open. "Tell me about Lexa Windham."

He gave his head a shake, trying to get all the facts before him to fall into place. "Wait. Who did you say you were? Why is the FBI here?"

Hernandez sighed and leaned back in her chair. She pulled a business card out of her pocket and pushed it across the table to Morgan. "Special Agent Danielle Hernandez. FBI."

He picked up the card. "Okay. I still don't understand why the FBI would be involved here."

One of Hernandez's eyebrows arched and her lips tightened. For a second, Morgan didn't think she was going to answer him. Then something changed in her eyes. In a somewhat gentler tone, she said, "The attack on Lexa Windham was the second attack on a hospital employee in Washington D.C. in two days. The responding officers noted some similarities between the two cases and thought it would be wise to call the Bureau in."

Morgan sank back in his chair. "Second attack? Who else was attacked?"

"A woman named Michelle Schultz was murdered night before last. She was a laboratory technician at Bridgepoint Hospital." Hernandez's gaze never left Morgan's face as she explained. What was she looking for? What kind of reaction?

Why did what she said about another woman being attacked ring a bell? Right. The newscast he'd had on as background noise as he'd sat in his apartment feeling sorry for himself. A flush of shame crept up his cheeks. How sadly self-indulgent he'd been. Who cared about what was happening to his marriage while Lexa had been fighting for her life? "Oh. I saw something on the news about that. What does it have to do with Lexa?"

Hernandez gave him a tight-lipped smile. "That's exactly what we're trying to figure out." She leaned forward, dark eyes boring into his. "Did you have any kind of conflict with Lexa? Any reason you'd want her out of the way."

Morgan shoved back in his chair so hard that he nearly toppled over backward. "What? No! Absolutely not. Lexa is an amazing resident. One of the best and brightest I've seen."

Now Hernandez's eyes narrowed. "Dr. Stark, were you romantically involved with Lexa?"

Seriously? Why was this where everyone's minds went? "Again, absolutely not. She's my resident. I enjoy working with her. She . . . she reminds me of my sister."

Hernandez made a note on her legal pad. "Okay, then. What about other people at the hospital? Is there anybody who was jealous of Lexa? Anyone she locked horns with?"

Morgan wracked his brains. Had he seen Lexa arguing with anyone? No. She'd generally been too busy to get into pissing matches with anyone. "Look. The medical field is competitive. There's a chance there's someone out there who resents Lexa for the spot she got in the program, but not enough to harm her. What would be the point of that? It doesn't make sense."

"You'd be surprised how little sense violence makes sometimes." Hernandez sighed. "What about patients? Anybody angry with Lexa about their treatment? It's a possibility that the attacker could be someone Lexa encountered while performing her duties at the hospital."

Morgan shook his head again. "No. Nothing that I can think of."

Hernandez made another note on her pad and then slipped it back into her briefcase. She pulled out his cell phone, wallet, and keys and pushed them across the table to him. "Well, thank you for your time, Dr. Stark. If you think of anything, please give me a call." She rose.

"Agent Hernandez?" Morgan asked.

"Yes?"

"How is Lexa? Where did they take her? I want to check on her progress." It would be touch and go, but Lexa was strong. Strong and smart. She'd be okay. She had to be okay. He couldn't allow himself to entertain any other possibility.

Hernandez sat back down and folded her hands in front of her. "No one's told you?"

"No. Every time I ask a question I'm told that they're the ones who get to do that." He could hear the frustration and resentment in his voice.

Hernandez shut her eyes for a moment and opened them slowly. "I'm sorry to have to tell you this, Dr. Stark. Lexa was pronounced dead at the scene."

Lexa dead? No. This couldn't be happening. This was a nightmare. White spots formed in front of Morgan's eyes and the room started to whirl around him. He gripped the edge of the table, willing himself back from the edge. It was unthinkable and yet he didn't believe this no-nonsense woman in front of him would be making up lies. As he grounded himself, one thought and one thought only gripped him. Whoever did this had to be caught and punished. "And you have no idea who did this?"

"We're working on developing leads."

Morgan knew what that meant. They had nothing.

He shoved back his chair and stood. He had to get out of here. He had to do something.

He had to see her. He had to see Lexa. He'd spent his entire professional life diagnosing illnesses based on things no one else seemed to notice. Maybe, if he saw her, he could find that one thing that no one else had seen that could crack this thing wide open.

"Where is she?" he asked.

Hernandez looked confused for a moment.

"Where is Lexa?" he demanded.

She stood. In heels she was nearly as tall as Morgan. She looked him directly in the eye and said, "She's at the Medical Examiner's. You'll have to wait until they've filed their report."

Wait for their report? He'd see about that.

CHAPTER SEVEN

Morgan stared up at the glass and concrete building before him. He'd never been to the District of Columbia's Office of the Chief Medical Examiner, or OCME as people referred to it. There'd never been a need. If he needed an autopsy report, he didn't tramp downtown to physically pick it up. He requested it through regular channels.

No way was he waiting for that now. There'd been a time that OCME had been infamous for its backlog of cases, bodies stacked up and waiting for months before an autopsy could be performed. That was no longer true, but it still could be as much as a 90-day wait for results.

Yesterday's rain had washed away the fog. The sun was almost painfully bright to Morgan's tired eyes as he walked into the lobby and looked around. He knew he looked like hell. By the time he'd walked out of the police station, it had been morning already. He'd come straight here. He was still in scrubs and the borrowed sweatshirt. He should probably have gone home, showered, changed clothes. It had seemed impossible, though. How could he just go home? There had to be more that he could do.

He took a second to get oriented and then strode up to the security guard on duty at a desk.

"I need to go to the morgue," he said without preamble.

The guard looked up from behind his desk, clearly unimpressed. "And you are?" A white guy in his late forties, the guard had the billowing middle and puffy features of an athlete who'd allowed himself to go to seed.

Morgan pulled out his ID badge and flashed it in front of the guard. "Dr. Morgan Stark. Georgetown University Hospital." He was pretty sure he could outrun this guy to get where he wanted to go, but that seemed counter-productive.

"They expecting you?" The guard picked up the phone like he was about to call someone.

"Yes. It's about a homicide case that would have been brought in this morning." Morgan brazened it out.

"This morning?" The guard put the phone back down. "They won't be getting to that today."

Morgan took a step back and gave a quick glance to the framed photographs on the wall of the office's personnel and then at the guard's badge. "Fine. Shall I tell Dr. Morris that I was unable to meet him because Stan wouldn't allow me to go up to the morgue?" He'd listened to enough imperious doctors to know how to sound like one.

The guard's lips tightened and he looked like he wanted to argue, but then he sighed. He picked up the phone and dialed. "I've got a Dr. Stark here to see Dr. Morris. Says it's about a homicide." He listened for a moment. "Says he's from Georgetown University Hospital." He listened again and then hung up. "Fine. Fifth floor." He handed Morgan a Visitor's badge and waved him through.

Morgan didn't wait a second before pushing through the turnstile and going to the elevator bank. He didn't want to give anyone a chance to change their mind. When he got off on the fifth floor, a bearded and bespectacled Black man in a rumpled gray suit was waiting for him, a slightly quizzical look on his face. "Hello, Dr. Stark. I'm Richard Morris. Did we have an appointment?"

Morgan debated what tack to take and then decided to go with honesty. "No. We didn't. A colleague was brought in this morning. She was the victim of a homicide. I . . . I was hoping to see her body in case there was something I might find that could help."

Morris's face creased. "I'm sorry for your loss, but are you working on the case somehow?"

Morgan shook his head. "I'm the one who found her." The words clogged in his throat. He looked down at his hands as if Lexa's blood might still be there.

Morris looked Morgan up and down and then indicated the path down the hallway with a head tilt. "Let's talk in my office."

The office was neater and tidier than Morgan expected. Certainly neater than his own. It was small, but had a window that looked out onto E Street. Morris took a seat behind the desk and indicated that Morgan should sit in one of the two chairs in front of the desk. He pulled a computer monitor around and tapped a few keys. "What was your colleague's name?"

"Lexa Windham." Morgan leaned forward in the chair, elbows braced on knees.

"Twenty-five-year-old white female?" Morris asked.

It was the barest description of everything that Lexa had been that it hurt to hear her described that way. This man had never met her, though. He'd never experienced her quick mind, her compassion for her patients. Morgan couldn't expect for him to identify her another way. "That's her."

Morris leaned back in his chair and crossed his arms over his chest. "The FBI has put a rush on her autopsy, but it's still not likely to happen until tomorrow. What is it exactly that you want here, Dr. Stark?"

Morgan rubbed his hand over his face. "I'm not entirely certain myself. I just know I have to see her. I have to find a way to help."

"And you think viewing her body will somehow let you accomplish that?" Morris sounded skeptical.

"It's possible." How could he explain to this man that his entire professional life had been about noticing the things that no one else did? "I have to try."

Morris made a bit of a face then seemed to come to a decision. He pushed himself back from his desk. "Come on then. She'll be in the body storage area pending tomorrow's autopsy."

They walked down the hallway, passing extra wide sliding glass doors. The buzz of the fluorescent lights made Morgan's temple begin to throb. He rubbed at it. The last thing he needed right now was a migraine.

Finally, they reached a door whose metal plaque read Body Storage. Morris waved his badge in front of the RFID reader and the doors opened. "She should be in 32 J."

The white tile floor was spotless. The walls were painted a pale, institutional green with glass-enclosed cabinets in each corner, like a doctor's office. The room was silent except for the hum of the lights and the ticking of a clock on the wall.

Morris strode to a bank of metal cabinet doors and located the one he wanted. He turned back to Morgan. "Are you sure about this? As a doctor, I'm sure you're used to viewing bodies, but it can be different when it's someone we know."

Morgan nodded. He'd spent more than twenty years dealing with bodies, living and dead. You had to be able to distance yourself from their humanity if you were going to do your job as a physician. It had never been a problem for him. In fact, sometimes he worried that he was a little too good at it. "I'll be fine."

Morris unlocked the cabinet and slid the gurney out. The body was covered with a sheet. He peeled it back off Lexa's face.

And it was Lexa's face. Not the face of a stranger. Not the face of a cadaver. Not the face of another body. It was her face. Her beautiful young face that would never look with kindness at another patient or crease while she thought through a tricky diagnosis. She would never laugh again, never cry. Morgan's eyes clouded with tears and, for a moment, it wasn't Lexa he saw, but Fiona. He'd never had this moment with his sister, never gotten closure. One day she'd been there. The next she'd been gone. He'd never gotten to say good-bye.

He motioned for Morris to fold the sheet down further, exposing the ugly gash across Lexa's throat and the bruises on her wrists. Even as his emotions whirled, his mind catalogued the marks and injuries on her body. The bruised wrists. The broken fingernails. The scraped knees.

He'd been wrong. It was too much. He couldn't stay here. He kissed his fingers and then pressed them against Lexa's forehead. It was so cold, so terribly, terribly cold.

A sob escaped him. Morris quickly pulled the sheet back up and slid Lexa back into the cabinet. Morgan grabbed onto the wall as he felt his knees go slightly weak when the latch clicked.

"Do you need to sit down? Have a glass of water?" Morris asked.

Morgan shook his head. "No. I . . . I just need to go. I was wrong. I have nothing to add here."

Morris walked him to the elevators and Morgan made his way back to the lobby, past the surly security guard, out of the building, and then to his car. The brisk air cut through his borrowed sweatshirt and he was shivering by the time he got in the Altima. He glanced at the clock. It was only 9 a.m. He had an entire day still ahead of him. He switched on the engine and headed to his apartment. He needed a hot shower and a fresh set of clothes.

But then what?

Work?

No. His mind reeled at the thought of walking the halls without Lexa there, of having to explain to people what had happened. He didn't think he could handle it. No one would expect it of him.

Stay at the apartment then?

And do what? Watch television? Day drink? Now it was his stomach that churned.

Fine. He'd take a quick shower and then get to the hospital.

The traffic was beastly. Stop and go. Interminable and boring, yet requiring his constant attention. Maybe that was good. Maybe the distraction was what he actually needed. He felt a little more in control of himself when he finally got back to his apartment.

Not having the energy to take the stairs or the will to face another stairwell, he took the elevator up. At the door, he dropped his keys. He made a pot of coffee and poured himself a mug and carried it into the bathroom with him.

He turned the shower handle to as hot as he could stand it and got in to let the water pour over him, hoping it would take away some of the chill that seemed to have seeped deep down into his bones. He shut his eyes, but all he could see was Lexa's cold pale face. His knees stung and he looked down, surprised to see scrapes across them. He frowned. Hadn't the ones on Lexa's knees been nearly identical?

He got out of the shower to inspect them more carefully. Where would he have gotten those? He cast his mind over the last twenty-four hours.

The only time he'd been on his knees was when he'd knelt next to Lexa's body and attempted CPR. He should have known it was fruitless. He would have if he'd let himself look at what had been done to her. Maybe it was a blessing in its own way that he'd been so consumed with trying to help her that he hadn't looked too closely.

He had now, though, and Lexa had the same scrapes on her knees. Where the hell would they have come from? The scrapes had to be from within the last twenty-four hours. They were much too fresh to be any older than that.

He wrapped a towel around his waist and went to his bedroom to get dressed, automatically pulling out dress slacks and a button-down shirt and a tie. He brushed his sandy brown hair – that needed to be trimmed – and finished his coffee. Then he gathered his wallet and keys and other items and headed back out the door to go to the hospital.

On the drive to the hospital, his mind kept returning to the scrapes on Lexa's knees. When would she have knelt down on a rough surface like that? Not out in that alleyway. She'd been dragged there, fighting all the way.

He pulled into his parking spot in the hospital garage and got out of the car, opting to take the stairs instead of the slow elevator. He entered the stairwell and it hit him.

What about the stairwell at Lexa's apartment building? Based on the smears of blood he'd seen, that was where she'd been attacked in the first place. He'd been in a hurry when he'd gone through there, focused mainly on finding Lexa. His mind, however, had a way of cataloging information no matter where his focus was.

There'd been the smear of blood, but there had also been blood up on the landing. What if Lexa had seen someone in trouble, someone bleeding on the landing and had stopped to help them? She would have knelt down next to the person. The concrete in the stairwell was rough and could have easily scraped her knees through her slacks.

So what had happened to the person? Where had they gone? Why hadn't they tried to help Lexa when she was attacked?

He froze. Unless the injured person was the attacker. He shook his head. No. Someone who had lost that much blood wouldn't have had the strength to attack Lexa and drag her out to the alleyway. She was a young strong woman. Based on her broken fingernails and the bruises on her wrists, she had definitely fought back.

Unless the person wasn't really injured. Agent Hernandez had said this was the second medical professional in as many days to be killed in a similar manner. How better to lure someone in health care into a vulnerable position than pretending to be injured yourself?

It made sense. If Lexa had seen someone she thought was in trouble, she would have dropped immediately to her knees to examine that person, just as he had.

He walked more slowly up the stairs, thinking about how that might have worked. He pushed open the heavy door and onto the floor. He'd stop by the nurses' station before he went to his office so they knew he was in. He rounded the corner and found Danielle Hernandez already there.

"Agent Hernandez, what are you doing here?"

"My job." She gave him a perfunctory smile. Today's suit was navy instead of black, but otherwise identical, her dark hair still pulled back in a low ponytail. "Interviewing people, trying to find out more about Lexa. You'd be surprised how often we find the perpetrator of a crime by really digging into the life of the victim."

Since she was here, he might as well pass on what he'd figured out. "Speaking of that, I, uh, went to the morgue and viewed Lexa's body after I left the police station this morning. I noticed something. I'm not sure if it'll be helpful or not."

She looked at him with that cool level gaze, assessing, measuring. "Right now, I'm open to any and all information," Hernandez said finally.

He gestured for her to follow him. "Let's go to my office. I'll explain."

"So how did you manage to get into the morgue?" she asked, as they walked down the corridor.

He felt color creeping up his cheeks. "I sort of bluffed my way in. I felt like I needed to see her. To really understand that she was gone."

They went through the waiting area and Morgan waved to the receptionist, then into the suite of offices and exam rooms. He unlocked the door to his office and they went in. He gestured to one of the chairs for her to take a seat and then sat down behind his desk.

Hernandez nodded. "I've seen how that works before, how sometimes people need to really see someone to know they're gone." She crossed her legs and picked a little piece of lint off her sharply creased trousers. "So what was it that you noticed while you were there?"

"Lexa had some scrapes on her knees. I didn't think too much about them until I got home and got in the shower and realized I had the exact same scrapes. I got mine when I knelt down in the alleyway to do CPR. I think she might have gotten them when she knelt down in the stairwell to help someone. There was a pool of blood on the landing above where it looked like Lexa was attacked."

Hernandez smiled slightly. "Actually, not blood. According to the lab, it looks like it was a mixture of cornstarch, corn syrup, cocoa, and red food coloring. In other words, fake blood. Something someone might make for Halloween. We haven't been able to figure out why it's there or if it's even connected."

Morgan scooted forward in his chair. That fit his hypothesis perfectly. "What if someone pretended to be injured to lure Lexa close enough to them to attack her?"

Hernandez's brow creased, but she uncrossed her legs and also scooted forward. "Explain."

Morgan took a moment to gather his thoughts. "If you wanted to get a nurse or doctor into a vulnerable position, the best way to do that would be to make them think you needed their help. That's all they'd be focused on. What the injury was, what to do to treat it. If the person wasn't actually injured, they'd be able to attack at that point without the nurse or doctor expecting it."

"So you think that someone played possum and used the fake blood to make her think they had a serious injury? Then when she stopped to help them, that person attacked her?" She tapped her index finger against her lower lip as she considered.

Morgan steepled his fingers in front of himself. "It fits all the things I'm seeing." It was like making a diagnosis. He'd taken all the different pieces, some of them seemingly unrelated, and shifted and turned them until they'd coalesced into a picture that he could recognize and understand.

It was tremendously satisfying and if it brought Danielle even one step closer to finding the bastard who'd killed Lexa, it would go a long way to soothing the hole in his heart that losing her had created.

"Indeed it does." Hernandez tilted her head to one side and gave him a long considering look. "You have an amazing attention to detail."

Morgan shrugged. "I need to have an attention to detail to do my job well."

"A lot of people need it, but they don't all have it," Hernandez said, wryly. "Some of my fellow agents don't have those kinds of observational skills."

It wasn't anything Morgan hadn't heard before. He'd always been able to take in details that others missed and keep them catalogued in his brain. Still, it never hurt to be recognized. "Thanks."

"If Lexa's murder is truly connected to Michelle Schultz's murder – and I am convinced they are – it means someone is targeting medical professionals. We could really use someone on the team who understands how the medical system works and what makes the people who do this work tick. No one at the Bureau came up with what you just figured out." She paused, those dark eyes watching him, calculating.

Morgan wasn't sure what she was getting at. "What are you suggesting?"

"Would you be willing to consult with the Bureau on this investigation?" She sat back again in her chair.

"Consult?" For the FBI? How would that even work?

"Yes. Give your expertise. Lend us that keen eye for observation. Help us wrap this case up before anyone else gets hurt."

It was so out of left field that Morgan couldn't quite grasp what she was saying. Him? Consult with the FBI? He was a doctor at a major hospital. He barely had time to eat most days, much less play around with law enforcement. Plus, based on his reaction to viewing Lexa's body that morning, he wasn't sure he could handle it. He shook his head. "I'm sorry. I don't think that's a good idea."

“Why not?” She was clearly disappointed.

He shook his head. “I’m already too emotionally involved in what’s happened here. I doubt I would be much good to you.”

“Don’t sell yourself short. You’ve already been a huge help.” She paused for a moment. “Sometimes emotional involvement isn’t all bad. It focuses you. You care.”

That feeling that he’d had standing over Lexa’s body in the morgue came back, the way her face merged with Fiona’s. He couldn’t do it. “I’m sorry, but no.”

Hernandez stood up and straightened her trouser legs. “Well, let me know if you change your mind. Thank you for what you’ve given me so far.”

Morgan watched her walk out the door and then turned to the files on his desk. He sighed, trying to work up the energy to tackle them. There was no spark in him when he looked at the work before him. He’d felt a glimmer of one when Danielle had told him his theory fit what she’d been seeing.

Maybe saying no to her offer wasn’t the right choice. He hoped he hadn’t just made a huge mistake.

CHAPTER EIGHT

Danielle sat in her FBI-issued Chevy Impala outside the house where Lexa Windham grew up in Bethesda. It was a split-level mid-century modern house. Nice, but not too special.

She'd spent the morning talking to Windham's colleagues. No one liked to speak ill of the dead, but everyone seemed to truly love Lexa. Well, almost everyone. Danielle had detected a few sour notes here and there from a few colleagues. Probably what Stark had said. They were jealous of the position Lexa had risen to, but that was hardly a motive for murder. Besides, what did it have to do with Michelle Schultz? She'd been a lab tech. A good job, but hardly one that inspired the kind of jealousy that would lead someone to murder.

She hadn't gotten much else useful from her morning at the hospital. Well, except for her conversation with Morgan Stark. That little detail about the scrapes on Lexa's knees was more than interesting. She'd have to check the crime scene notes on Michelle's file to see if there was anything similar. She sighed. What else might that man notice that would get past other people? Danielle was sure he could be key in wrapping up the investigation. It frustrated the hell out of her that he'd refused to get on board.

Danielle opened the door of the car and got out. Squaring her shoulders, she made her way up the flagstone sidewalk to the front door and rang the doorbell. Talking to bereaved families wasn't her favorite part of the job. At least she hadn't had to make the death notice. Those were brutal.

It had been bad enough to tell Morgan that Lexa hadn't made it. The anguish on his face had made her own heart clench. Then she'd watched as he pulled himself together and made an action plan. It was an impressive combination of emotional and intellectual intelligence. That was something that couldn't be taught. People had it or they didn't. She'd seen how it worked out in the field. Having someone like that on the team could mean the difference between breaking a case and having it be one of those that haunted you as you tried to fall asleep at night.

Damn. She really wished he hadn't rejected her idea of him consulting on the case so quickly. She slipped her sunglasses off and tucked them in the pocket of her trench coat.

Through the narrow windows on either side of the door, she saw a middle-aged white woman coming toward her. She was a big woman, tall and blonde and busty. She'd probably been a brickhouse when she was young, but she'd gone soft around the middle as she aged. The woman opened the door a crack. "Yes?"

Danielle flashed her badge. "Mrs. Windham, I'm Special Agent Danielle Hernandez with the FBI. I was hoping we could talk about your daughter."

The woman's face crumpled. She dabbed at her eyes with a tissue and nodded, opening the door wider to allow Danielle in. "Sorry," she whispered.

Danielle had seen a lot of grief, but it never got easy. If it ever did, she should probably leave the job. She knew agents who became so obsessed with the puzzle presented by the investigation that they forgot the very human wreckage that had brought them into the picture at all. They forgot why they were doing what they did.

One look at Lexa Windham's mother's face would remind anyone of what lay at the heart of this investigation.

A young woman, gone way too soon, before she could even begin to fulfill her potential.

"Thank you," Danielle said and followed Katja Windham into the house. It was light and airy with a vaulted ceiling in the living room and a dining room that had windows onto a little courtyard.

"Can I get you a cup of coffee? Some water?"

Danielle shook her head. "No. That's not necessary."

"How about a cookie?" Mrs. Windham walked into the kitchen. The counter was covered with covered casseroles and plates of sweets. "People keep bringing things. I guess they don't know what to do so they cook and bake. We'll never be able to eat it all."

"A cookie would be great," Danielle said, choosing a snickerdoodle from a plate that Mrs. Windham had picked up.

"Hold on. I'll get my husband." Windham left the kitchen.

Danielle could hear the murmur of voices, although she couldn't quite make out what they were saying. Everything felt subdued. She ate a bite of the cookie, but it felt dry in her mouth. She didn't think it was really about the cookie. It was more about the heaviness of the grief that had settled in the house. She wrapped the cookie in a napkin and put it in her pocket. Who knew? Maybe she'd get desperate later and want to eat it. She'd certainly had days on duty when there'd been no time to eat and she would have been grateful for half a stale cookie.

Katja Windham returned followed by her husband. He was taller and broader than his wife, with thinning dark hair. His face had the same hollowed out expression as his wife's. He stuck out his hand. "Gabriel Windham."

Danielle introduced herself again. "Could we sit down?" she asked.

Katja shook her head. "Of course. I'm sorry. I don't know where my head is." Then she led the way into the living room. The Windhams sat next to each other on the couch, hands clasped together. For some couples, the death of a child drove a wedge between them. Others turned to each other for support. It looked like the Windhams were part of the latter group. Danielle was unaccountably glad. She didn't know much about Lexa Windham yet, but she was relatively sure that the last thing the young woman would have wanted was to break up her parents' long marriage.

"So why is the FBI involved in my daughter's death?" Gabriel asked.

Danielle looked down at her hands. Sometimes people didn't understand enough about law enforcement to know when it was unusual to have the FBI called in. Sometimes they watched enough TV to realize there were jurisdictional issues. "There's a possibility that Lexa's death is linked to another one in D.C."

"Another death? Whose?" Katja leaned forward. "When?"

Danielle pulled out a photo of Michelle Schultz. "Do you recognize this woman? Her name was Michelle Schultz. Were she and Lexa friends?" It would be great to find some link between Lexa and Michelle besides them both being female and working in health care. So far, nothing had come up. They didn't go to the same gym or the same hair salon. They hadn't gone to the same school or participated in the same sports. "Did Lexa ever mention her? Or bring her by the house?"

Katja took the photo from Danielle and looked at it carefully, then shook her head. She passed the photo to her husband who also shook his head. Katja passed the photo back. "Sorry. I don't recognize her. Is she the one who worked at Bridgepoint? The one that was on the news?"

Danielle slipped the photo back into her breast pocket. "Yes. That's her."

“What ties her to Lexa?” Gabriel asked.

“I really can’t comment further on an ongoing investigation. I promise I will tell you what I can, when I can. Right now, I’m trying to find out more about who Lexa was to see if I can find any reason for why this happened.”

Gabriel rubbed his free hand across his face. “It has to have been random. Lexa was . . . she was . . .” He put his hand over his eyes and stopped speaking.

“She was brilliant,” her mother picked up the thread. “She knew she wanted to be a doctor from the time she was seven. She’d had her appendix out and she found the whole thing fascinating. Couldn’t stop asking questions. Wanted to see everything. She worked so hard at school. And she’d gotten such a prestigious residency at Georgetown. Her life was just beginning. I still can’t believe that some maniac cut it short.”

Pretty much the same thing all her colleagues at Georgetown had said. “Did Lexa have any enemies?”

Katja looked confused for a second, as if she didn’t understand the question. “No,” she said. “No enemies. Lexa wasn’t that kind of person.”

“She had to be at least a little bit competitive to get where she was,” Danielle said, carefully. “Maybe she stepped on some toes on her way up?”

“She was more focused than competitive,” Gabriel said.

Danielle understood that, although she also knew all too well that it didn’t mean people didn’t resent you.

“How is Dr. Stark?” Katja asked.

“Morgan Stark?” Danielle asked, eyes widening a bit. Was there more to that relationship than Stark had let on? “He’s upset. Sad. But okay. Why do you ask?”

“Lexa thought so highly of him. Talked about how brilliant he was all the time. He seemed to have taken a real interest in her.” Katja paused. “Nothing creepy, mind you. Like a mentor.”

That sounded about right.

“I just hope he’s okay,” Katja said.

“I’m sure he is.” Okay, but not willing to help her out on this case. Danielle gathered her things and said good-bye to the Windhams. Back at her car, she checked her notebook, deciding where to proceed next. Morgan Stark. She shook her head. He knew Lexa Windham better than anyone, maybe even better than her own parents. He was so damn observant, too. And logical. The leap he'd made from the scrapes on Lexa's knees to the idea of someone luring her into an ambush was spot on.

Why wouldn't he help? He could be the key to wrapping the whole case up. Danielle glanced at her watch. It was after five. Maybe he'd be home. She'd take one last run at convincing him. She turned the key and the engine purred to life.

CHAPTER NINE

Morgan was anything but okay.

He'd come damn close to making a significant mistake today. He'd almost missed a case of sepsis in one of his patients. He didn't know where his head had been. Certainly not analyzing Reta Shuman's white blood cell count or procalcitonin levels with any accuracy. Luckily, Ayres – of all people – caught it before significant damage was done. He'd clapped Morgan on the back and said something about good turns and everyone making mistakes and had walked away. No gloating. Morgan had misjudged the man and he was damn grateful that Ayres had been there today.

Reta could easily have died.

But Ayres couldn't be there every day and the miscalculation shook Morgan. Hard. He'd never made that kind of error before. So he'd marched into his office and fired off an email informing the hospital he'd be taking a leave of absence, effective immediately.

Now he was back in the worn recliner chair in his depressing apartment with an extremely good glass of Scotch. He took a sip, appreciating the way the smoky taste lingered on his tongue.

His cell phone rang. He glanced at the Caller ID and sighed. It was Ashley.

He might as well answer. It wasn't likely the day was going to get any worse. He hadn't done a damn thing about getting those papers signed and notarized. She'd made it clear that he needed to do it and he'd pushed it to the very bottom of his to-do list. He'd be frustrated with himself if he was her. He'd do it tomorrow. He'd have time, after all. "Hi, Ashley."

"Morgan, are you okay?"

Of course, she wasn't calling him to berate him for not getting that paper notarized. She was calling to check on him. Word got around the administrative offices fast. She'd clearly heard about his leave of absence. She'd been right to leave him. She was too good for him.

"I've been better." He took another sip of the Scotch.

"I heard that you've taken a leave of absence. What's going on?"

"Did you hear about Lexa?"

There was a pause. "I did. Tragic. She was your resident?"

He set down the Scotch and pushed back in the recliner. "Maybe the best I'd ever seen. Nearly as smart as Fiona."

He heard Ashley's little intake of breath. Fiona might be on his mind nearly constantly, but he almost never uttered her name.

"Morgan, are you sure you're all right?"

What good would it do to tell Ashley the truth? No. He wasn't all right. All right wasn't even visible in his rearview mirror. He poured another finger or two of Scotch. "I'm fine, Ash. I just needed some time to process it all and I didn't want my patients to suffer while I was distracted."

"You're sure?"

"When have I ever been anything less than 100% sure?" He tried to inject his words with his usual cockiness. It rang hollow to his ears.

She laughed. "So true. You have always had the courage of your convictions."

He smiled and then felt it crumble from his face. Hadn't he told Lexa that was what she needed? And now she'd never get a chance to develop that.

"Thanks for calling, Ashley, but I'll be fine."

"Okay." Another pause. "Call if you need anything?"

"Of course." He hung up and dropped his head in his hands. What would happen if he called her back right now and said the one thing he needed was her? He needed her supple lavender-scented arms and her smooth skin. He needed her soft, almost shy kiss. He needed the oblivion he knew he could find when she held him.

It wasn't fair, though. He couldn't lay that on her. Not now. If he was honest with himself, not ever.

A sharp three knocks sounded on his door. He frowned at it. He wasn't expecting anyone. It must be a mistake.

Three knocks again. This time louder.

Probably a pizza delivery for someone down the hall. Damn kids were generally so high they couldn't read the apartment numbers. He got up to answer the door and send whoever it was on their merry way.

But it wasn't a pizza delivery person. It was Special Agent Danielle Hernandez, looking every bit as cool and neat as she had when he'd seen her this morning in the police station and later at the hospital. It didn't even look like there was a hair escaping her ponytail.

"Special Agent Hernandez. How did you get into the building?" If you didn't have a key, you had to be buzzed in.

She smiled and moved her jacket aside so he could see her badge. "The badge opens a lot of doors."

"I can see that." She was here, after all.

"May I come in?"

He looked back over his shoulder as if there might be something he didn't want her to see. Sadly, his existence was pathetic enough that there wasn't a thing here that the FBI would care about. He stepped back. "Of course."

They walked into the living room. "Scotch?" he asked, holding up the bottle.

She shook her head and smiled. "Not at the moment. Thanks." She took a seat on the couch, adjusting her slacks as she sat. She leaned forward, elbows braced on knees. "I've come to ask you to reconsider."

"Reconsider what?" He thought he knew, but best to be sure they were on the same page.

"Working with me on this case." She looked him directly in the eye, unflinching. "I need your help. I'm hitting nothing but dead ends here. I feel it in my bones that having you working with me would change all that. You know the medical field. You know how hospitals work. Most importantly, you knew Lexa, perhaps better than anyone else."

Morgan poured more Scotch into his glass, sloshing it slightly. Damn it. "No."

"That's it? Just no? No reason?"

"I have a million reasons. I'm . . . I'm not in a good place. I doubt I'd be much good to anyone for any reason." His life had come apart, but it was hardly any of Danielle Hernandez's business.

Her lips tightened. "Really? Do you think you're the only person who ever got divorced?"

He looked up sharply. "How did you know about my divorce?"

She sat back on the couch, stretching her arms across its back. "It's not exactly top secret. Five minutes of hanging around the hospital cafeteria eavesdropping got me that."

He frowned. It hadn't occurred to him that he'd be the subject of gossip, but it made sense. He and Ashley had been a golden couple. Him in the trenches. Her in admin and public policy. They'd been highly visible. People loved to watch stuff like that implode. Schadenfreude.

"You're already on a leave of absence." She sighed, "So what is it that you're going to do if you don't help me? Sit in this exquisitely appointed apartment and drink?" She looked around at the bare walls and tattered furniture.

She had a point. What was he going to do? How long could he wallow in his disappointment and grief? What would it get him if he did? "What would I do if I helped you?"

A hint of a smile played at the corner of her lips, but she was smart enough to keep it from being a full triumphant grin. "Tag along with me. Use that keen eye to pick up details I'm missing. Help me understand hospital politics and procedure."

It didn't sound so bad. It might even be interesting. And if he helped catch the bastard who had killed Lexa? Well, they'd better not leave him alone with whoever it was. It might give his life some purpose, something that had been missing for a long time. He thought it was on the verge of returning as he'd worked with Lexa. Seeing her learn and grow. Helping her become the amazing doctor she was destined to be. It had brought some joy back to what he'd done that had disappeared long ago.

Maybe her death could help give him some purpose, too. "When would we start?"

Danielle stood. "Tomorrow morning. First thing. Meet me at FBI Headquarters downtown. We'll hit the ground running."

CHAPTER TEN

The next morning, Morgan took the Metro to the Federal Triangle Station and walked the five minutes to the J. Edgar Hoover Building on Pennsylvania Avenue. It wasn't much. Typical for the era during which it was built, it was a great example of American Brutalism. In other words, it was ugly. Squat. Low. Blocky. Clouds seemed to press down on it, making it look even more menacing.

Was he doing the right thing here? This was a different world than the one he was used to. Danielle was right. He knew medicine. He knew hospitals. What did he know about law enforcement? Or the FBI? How much would he really be able to contribute?

There was only one way to find out.

Morgan joined the line of people waiting to enter the building and pulled up the collar of his fleece jacket against the morning breeze. The chill was back in the air. It was supposed to rain before the afternoon. He'd probably be on his way home before then.

Finally, it was his turn to enter the building and go through the metal detector, emptying his pockets of keys and change and money clip and retrieving everything on the other side. He froze for a second, overwhelmed by the giant seal on the floor that proclaimed the fidelity, bravery, and integrity with which the Federal Bureau of Investigation operated. He skirted around it. It seemed wrong to step on it. He tried to nail down the unfamiliar emotion he was experiencing.

Oh. Nerves. It had been a while since he'd felt that!

He told the Black woman in her early forties behind the security desk that he was there to see Danielle Hernandez and then stepped back. "You got an appointment?"

"She's expecting me," he answered.

She stared at him for a second, clearly unimpressed, then adjusted her blue uniform shirt. "ID, please."

He handed over his driver's license. She squinted down at it and then back up at him and then picked up the phone. "Morgan Stark down here to see you. Says you're expecting him." She listened for a moment and then nodded and hung up. She pointed to a padded bench against the wall. "You can wait there. She'll be down in a moment."

Morgan took a seat, letting his eyes wander over the flags – one for the Bureau and one for the United States. Across from him was the Wall of Honor with photos and commemorations of fallen FBI agents. He swallowed hard. These people had given their lives to save others. That was a lot to live up to.

"Hi, Morgan." Danielle stood before him, holding out a Visitor's Badge. "You'll need this."

He looped it around his neck and stood. Too late for second thoughts now. "Thanks."

She had a funny look on her face.

"What?" he asked, checking to make sure his fly was zipped or if he had something hanging from his nose.

"I don't think I've seen you in jeans. You've always been in scrubs or a suit." She motioned for him to follow her and started walking.

"I'm not sure the last time I wore them," he admitted as he went through the turnstile after her, giving a little wave and smile of thanks to the security guard who nodded at him in return. "Scrubs or suits pretty describes the parameters of my life."

Danielle gave a little snort, pushing the button on the elevator. "I hear you. I think I have suits and work out gear."

Apparently Agent Hernandez needed to get a life nearly as much as Morgan did.

Up on the fourth floor, Danielle touched her badge to the RFID reader to open the door into the Behavioral Analysis Unit and they walked into a big open room that housed desks and cubicles. About half the desks were occupied. Men. Women. Black. White. Asian. Latino.

"Come this way," Danielle said. "I have us set up in one of the conference rooms."

The room was smaller and darker. File folders were scattered across the round table in the center and a laptop was plugged into a surge protector whose cord ran across the floor. He'd heard the building was outdated and a new headquarters was being proposed. He understood why now.

Two walls were taken up with boards. One had a photo of Lexa in the top left corner. The other had a photo of a woman who looked vaguely familiar. Of course. Michelle Schultz. The other victim.

The two looked a little bit alike. Both had dark hair parted in the middle and light skin. Both were in their twenties. Did their killer have a type?

Each board had a timeline. Lexa's showed what time she'd left the hospital and when she'd crossed various traffic cameras on her way home, her call to Morgan, and when Morgan had found her. Michelle's had much the same. They'd both left their respective hospitals late and the times they left didn't correspond to normal shift changes. That made sense with Lexa. Residents worked all kinds of hours. A lab tech should have been more on a regular schedule, though. Why was Michelle out so late?

Each board also had photos of the two crime scenes. Morgan took a moment to inwardly steel himself before looking at those. It didn't help. Sorrow threatened to swamp him as he looked at Lexa's staring eyes and slack jaw. He turned away.

"Careful there." Danielle gestured at the cord to her laptop as she took a seat. Morgan sat down across from her. "I thought we could start with reviewing the files on Michelle and Lexa to see if we can find any commonalities."

"Besides that they were both women working in health care in Washington, D.C., and looked a bit alike?" Morgan asked. "There are probably hundreds of people who would fit that description. How sure are we that the killings are even related?"

"Well, there's the cause of death. They both had their throats slit." She shoved the folder for Michelle across the table to him. "If we had any questions about it, what you noticed probably erased them. Look at her knees."

Morgan flipped to the autopsy report, although he knew what he would see. The same scrapes as had been on Lexa's knees and that were on his own. He blew out a breath. "So somebody lured Michelle to them as well? By pretending to be injured?"

Danielle leaned back in her chair and stretched. "We think so. We checked Michelle's cell phone. Wanna guess who her last call was to?"

Morgan shook his head. Guessing wasn't really his bag. Deducing from a set of facts? Sure. Not guessing, though.

"911. She called to report an injured man in an alleyway close to where she was found. We hadn't realized the two things were connected until you pointed out that thing about Lexa's knees." Danielle tapped the file folder. "No one was looking for the site of a fake injury when we first investigated the crime scene. He dragged Lexa away from the place he ambushed her. It makes sense that he would have done the same to Michelle. We've got people looking now, but it might be too late to find whatever he staged."

"So it's definitely a man."

"Statistically it makes sense. Serials are generally men. Especially in cases like these where the unsub seems to be hunting victims. Plus it would have taken a certain amount of strength to drag Lexa and probably Michelle the way he did."

"Unsub?"

"Sorry. Jargon." She wrinkled her nose. "Unidentified subject."

"Right." It wasn't like his own profession didn't have a lot of jargon to it. The difference was that he knew that jargon. He'd been speaking it all of his adult life. What was he doing here? He didn't even speak these people's language. By the time he got up to speed, the case would be cold.

"What we're looking for is why these two? There are hundreds of young women with dark hair who work in health care in Washington D.C." Danielle leaned forward, dark eyes intense, and interlaced her fingers. "If we can find the nexus, the place that connects them, we may find the person who killed them or, at the very least, find their motive."

Okay. That he could do. Finding those connections was his specialty. Morgan shrugged out of the fleece jacket and hung it on the back of the office chair. He ran his hands over the folder. Then he flipped the folder back to its first page. The woman in the photo paperclipped to the first page of the report that greeted him still looked vaguely familiar. Then again, she'd been the lead story in pretty much every local newscast he'd caught in the past few days.

The name was familiar, too, though. "How long had Michelle worked at Bridgepoint?" he asked Danielle.

She flipped through a couple of pages and frowned. "Less than a year."

"Where'd she work before?" Morgan asked, fairly certain he knew the answer.

Danielle frowned down at the papers in front of her. "Georgetown."

Well, there was one step closer to that nexus Hernandez was seeking. Georgetown was a big place, though. He sat back and read the rest of the file, sliding into that focused mental space that let him connect the dots for a difficult diagnosis.

Lexa had grown up in Bethesda, near D.C., but had left to do her undergrad at UC Berkeley and then medical school at Rush University in Chicago. She'd made her way back to the east coast for her residency. She'd mentioned how happy she was to be close to her family again a couple of times.

Michelle had been born in D.C., had an Associate's degree from a technical college in D.C., and had worked at Howard University Hospital before she'd come to Georgetown and then had moved on to Bridgepoint. Based on her file, Morgan wasn't sure if she'd ever traveled more than a hundred miles from the District, much less lived on another coast.

Like a lot of residents, Lexa didn't have time for much in the way of hobbies, but she apparently made time to play piano now and then. Michelle was active in her church and was on a bowling team.

Lexa was single and wasn't dating anyone seriously. Michelle had recently moved in with her girlfriend of two years.

So much for his big brain. It wasn't helping. There was nothing obvious except that the two women had both worked at Georgetown at the same time. He leaned back in the desk chair, tapping his pen against the yellow pad where he'd been taking notes. They didn't work in the same department although every department sent stuff to the lab. Was that it? Could it be that simple?

"Okay," he said into the silence. "Hear me out."

Hernandez looked up from her computer. "Nothing I want more. Except maybe a decent cup of coffee." She tossed the paper cup she'd been sipping from off and on for the last hour into a garbage can.

He snorted. "What if Lexa and Michelle worked on the same case at some point? What if that's the connection? And what if that case didn't go well? Maybe there's a disgruntled patient out there taking revenge."

Danielle's eyes narrowed. "Establishing that would require combing through a lot of medical records."

Morgan shrugged. "I've got time on my hands."

"It would also be a hard sell to get a warrant that would allow us that access. Maybe if we had a specific request with a limited scope, but no way is a judge going to let us comb willy-nilly through people's medical records." She stood and went to the windows to adjust the blinds. It didn't help. The room was still dark.

Danielle couldn't necessarily get at those records, but he could. "I'm a doctor with privileges at Georgetown. I don't need a warrant to look at people's medical records."

"I'm pretty sure you have to have a reason to access them."

"Isn't solving two murders a good enough reason?" It was this kind of bureaucracy that drove him crazy. "What about possibly preventing more violence? There's no way that the only two people who worked on a case would be a lab tech and a resident. There'd be doctors and nurses and orderlies and nursing assistants. Who knows how many people might have been part of the care team? Who knows how many other people could be targets? Whoever this person is. I doubt that he's going to stop with Michelle and Lexa."

"That's not how this works. We compile evidence that we present to a judge to get a warrant. We want everything we find to be admissible in court." Danielle turned away from the window to face him.

Morgan threw up his hands. "How are we supposed to compile evidence if we're not allowed to look at anything?"

"We build our case bit by bit." Danielle looked at him with narrowed eyes. "I'm serious, Morgan. We have rules and protocols here just like you do in the hospital. They exist for a reason."

He sat back and sighed. "So what do I do now? I'm not sure there's anything more in these files to read over." When he'd arrived, he hadn't been sure if he should even be here. Now he didn't want to leave. There was something there, something more that he wasn't seeing. It felt just out of reach.

"You go home. Kick back. Have a glass of that incredibly stinky Scotch you were drinking the other night." Danielle shut the folder in front of her as well. "I'll get in touch as soon as we have any more information to work with."

"Not a fan of peat I take it." Morgan got up and put on his jacket, but his brain was going a million miles a minute. He got it. He really did. She had to do things by the book.

"Not that much peat!" She stood. "I appreciate all the work today. We're making progress. I can feel it."

He could too. That's part of what was so frustrating about her not letting him access those patient files.

Did he have to do things by the book? He wasn't so sure about that. Plus, whatever he found in those records wouldn't necessarily be evidence. It would send them in a direction to find evidence. Danielle could get as many warrants as she wanted for that.

Besides, what Danielle didn't know wouldn't hurt her.

CHAPTER ELEVEN

The rain had finally started. It had been threatening all day. Good timing as far as he was concerned. The water beading up on the car windows would give him extra cover. Plus, people didn't look around in the rain. They scurried from one place to another as if a little water was going to melt them.

Bunch of snowflakes.

Sure enough. Here she came. Umbrella angled to block out the wind. Her keys must have already been in her hand because he heard the double beep and the car's lights flashed as she unlocked it. She ducked inside, pulling the umbrella after her like a turtle retreating into its shell. If he hadn't already established that the car was hers, he might not have been sure it was her.

But he had. He'd done his homework. He'd combed through all the records and he knew all their names. From there, it had been relatively easy to find everything else he needed to know.

People were so stupid. Putting all their personal information out there for everyone to see on social media. Or if they didn't, their friends did and it was still ridiculously easy to figure it all out. This one's cohort at nursing school had posted almost every minute of their graduation two years before. Then it was a matter of following the trail through the Internet. He hadn't even had to leave his apartment to find out where she lived, who she lived with, what she drove, even what shift she was on.

She pulled out of her parking space. He gave her a second or two and then did the same. It was shift change time at Georgetown University Hospital so there were dozens of cars leaving all at once. Even if it hadn't been raining, he doubted she would notice him. He was one gray sedan in a line of gray sedans. In minutes, he was behind her on the road heading toward her home.

Stupid bitch. He was going to enjoy watching her face as she recognized him, as she connected him to what she'd done to his family in the name of medicine, as she realized that she was going to have to pay for what she did.

And then he'd slit her throat.

CHAPTER TWELVE

Morgan drove past the line of cars leaving the Georgetown University Hospital parking lot. How many gray sedans were there in this town? He'd taken the Metro home and picked up his car after he left Danielle at FBI Headquarters and then driven here to the hospital.

He'd battled with himself the whole way about what his next step was. He understood Danielle's concerns.

He just didn't think they outweighed his.

It was no longer only about revenge. He definitely wanted to see whoever had killed Lexa punished to the full extent of the law. He also didn't want anyone else to get hurt. He took his Hippocratic Oath seriously. First, do no harm. Standing by, knowing that someone might be targeting the staff at his hospital was definitely allowing harm to happen. How was he supposed to live with himself if someone else got hurt?

He parked his Altima and looped his hospital ID around his neck. Under the cover of his umbrella, he ducked into the hospital, then shook the rain off. He made his way up to his office, nodding occasionally at people he knew, but not stopping to talk. The less he had to say about why he was spending the first day of his leave of absence here at the hospital, the better.

That he was right about his instincts became abundantly clear when he got to his office.

"Dr. Stark?" Reem Ahmed, the Internal Medicine administrative assistant, half rose from behind his desk as Morgan walked by. "I . . . we . . . I mean, I didn't expect you in today."

The young man's dark cheeks turned a bit red.

Morgan raised a hand. "I didn't expect to be in myself, but I realized I needed to do a little bit of follow up on Reta Shuman." Shuman had been the sepsis case that Morgan had almost missed. He actually did want to make sure she was continuing to improve, but also figured she'd be a great case to use as cover.

Ahmed nodded. "Of course." He sat back down.

In his office, Morgan started up his computer and got settled behind his desk. This wasn't going to be easy or straightforward. First, he'd have to make a list of cases Lexa had worked on. He'd work backward from Vincenzo Rohr. She'd been working with him for three months. He'd start there and see if Michelle's name turned up on any of the lab reports.

He plunged into the list of cases and then through the reams of paperwork that came with each one. There were plenty of lab tests that had been run. It was standard protocol to test blood and urine from every patient when trying to make a diagnosis. Every patient he and Lexa had treated had those. Then there were specialized tests. Biopsies and tissue samples. The list was long.

He couldn't find a single case that Lexa had worked on with him that had Michelle's name on the lab work. That didn't necessarily mean that Michelle hadn't run any of the lab tests involved in those cases. The tech's name doesn't always appear on a test.

None of the cases Lexa had worked with him had turned out poorly, either, though. It had to be something where a case had gone wrong somehow. Why kill someone over them healing you or someone you loved? That made no sense.

He snorted. How much sense would the twisted mind behind all this make anyway?

He shut down that search and started another, checking Lexa's cases before she came onto his rotation. There was a soft knock at his door. "Come in."

Ahmed opened the door slightly and peeked in. "I'm leaving for the day, Dr. Stark. Is there anything I can get you before I go?"

Morgan glanced at the clock on his computer. Hours had gone by already. He shook his head. "No. Thank you, Reem. I appreciate it."

Reem withdrew, but paused before he shut the door. "I'm so sorry about Dr. Windham. She . . . she was wonderful to work with."

Morgan smiled. "She was, wasn't she? It's a great loss."

Ahmed nodded and then left, pulling the door shut so quietly there almost wasn't a click. Morgan sighed and went back to his search.

Maybe it was a case that Lexa had worked on before she'd started working with Morgan. Lexa had been a relatively new resident. She'd done only one rotation before coming to his department. Unluckily, it was the Emergency Department. That meant a lot of patients and a lot of tests to comb through. He got up from his desk, did some stretches and sat back down to work it through.

You didn't get through medical school, residency, and post-docs without developing an iron butt.

It was nearly ten o'clock before Morgan felt he had a list to start with. He'd found five cases that Lexa had run point on that Michelle had also run tests for.

Georgeanne Plunkett, a sixty-two-year-old white female, had been brought in by her husband with chest pains. Lexa had run an electrocardiogram or ECG, always the first test to run if you suspect a heart attack. Plunkett's heart muscles seemed to be conducting electrical impulses just fine, making the likelihood that she had or was having a heart attack highly unlikely. At the same time, however, Lexa had sent blood to the lab. That was where Michelle had come in. Michelle had run the test that hadn't turned up in of the proteins or enzymes a doctor would expect to find in the blood sample if the patient was having a heart attack. Plunkett did, however, have high cholesterol, high blood pressure, and elevated blood sugars. Lexa had recommended Plunkett follow up on those conditions with her primary care physician. They weren't exactly Emergency Department issues. They were chronic. In the end, Lexa had released Georgeanne Plunkett with a prescription for an antacid.

So where was Ms. Plunkett these days? Morgan pulled up her files, almost dreading what he'd find. Maybe Lexa had been wrong. Maybe Plunkett had been having or was about to have a heart attack. Maybe she'd ignored chest pains later because she thought they were nothing.

But no. Apparently not. Georgeanne Plunkett had taken Lexa's advice and talked to her primary care doc. As of her last doctor's appointment three weeks ago, she'd lost twenty-two pounds and her A1C was in an acceptable range. She was still fighting with the cholesterol and the blood pressure, but she was healthier for having had Lexa as her doctor and Michelle as her lab tech.

Cross her off the list.

He moved on to the next one. Twenty-seven-year-old road biking enthusiast, Sammie Womack, who'd had a close encounter with a vehicle on Skyline Drive. Lexa had sent him for a CT-Scan, X-rays and, once again, had sent blood work down to the lab where Michelle had been the tech on duty. It had been a good thing Womack had been wearing a helmet. He'd hit his head pretty hard, but there was no bleeding or indication of concussion. He had, however, broken his left arm. There'd been nothing notable in his blood work. There also wasn't much in his file. Morgan switched over to social media. It took him about ten minutes to find a photo of Sammie clad in spandex and proclaiming joy at being able to get back on his bike.

That was another one that didn't seem a likely person to take revenge.

The next case, however, held some possibilities. Paramedics had brought in thirty-two-year-old Cole Hutton and his seven-year-old daughter, Renee, to be treated for smoke inhalation. An untended candle had started a fire in their apartment. They'd been lucky to get out alive. It had actually been the daughter who'd heard the smoke alarm and woken her father.

Father and daughter both had had chest x-rays that were all clear, but Lexa had also sent blood samples to the lab to be sure she wasn't missing anything. The only thing she'd been missing was Cole's blood alcohol level—which was more than double the legal limit for driving—and the presence of Fentanyl.

Morgan remembered Lexa talking about this one. It had bothered her. The man had clearly endangered his child and Lexa was a mandatory reporter. Child Protective Services had been notified. She'd said the little girl's wails as she'd been taken away from her father had broken Lexa's heart. She'd asked Morgan what else she'd been supposed to do, if there'd been a way to handle it better.

There wasn't. Or, at least, not that Morgan knew. They saw a lot of people who'd made some bad decisions in the Emergency Department. Hutton was one more.

Morgan looked through the man's file to see if there was anyone who'd been there that he could talk to. He saw the names of two nurses that he had at least a passing familiarity with in the case notes. He looked up at the clock. It was after eleven. He did a quick search and found that one of them—Imani Thomas—was working in the Emergency Department right then.

He jotted down some notes and went to find her.

The Emergency Department was in its usual state of controlled chaos. He'd done the required rotations there as a resident, but it wasn't his scene. Morgan operated from a slight remove, observing and comparing and calculating. There wasn't time for that in an emergency. That was all about instinct and muscle memory.

It didn't hurt if you were a bit of an adrenaline junkie as well.

He spotted Imani coming out of a curtained-off bay. She was a light-skinned Black woman with graying braids piled up on top of her head. Even with the braids, she barely topped five foot four, though. He raised a hand to wave to her and get her attention.

Her steps slowed when she saw him. She gave him a quizzical smile and pointed to her chest as if to ask, "me?" Morgan smiled and nodded.

Imani tapped her watching and held up five fingers and then pointed to a consulting area off in the corner. He got the message.

Morgan settled in to wait. It was a little room with a desk, a computer terminal, a light box for viewing X-rays, and a few office chairs.

It was more like ten minutes, but Imani eventually came in and sat down across from him. "Dr. Stark, how can I help you?" Her voice had just a trace of an island lilt to it.

"I wanted to ask you about a patient named Cole Hutton."

She frowned. "I'm going to need a little more information than that. We get quite a few people through here. It's hard to remember every name." She gestured out to the floor where every bay was full.

"Right." He stroked his chin. How to remind her of who this guy was without giving her so much information that he influenced what she'd tell him? "He would have been through here about five months ago. We treated him for smoke inhalation. Him and his daughter. She was about seven."

Realization dawned on Imani's face. "Oh, yes. I remember that one. Broke everyone's heart, for sure, but there wasn't much to be done about it. As I recall, he was high as a kite and had nearly burned down their place around the daughter's ears. She was the one who got him out of the apartment, if memory serves."

Good. Her memory matched what Morgan had read in the chart. "CPS took the daughter?"

"Don't remember if it was CPS or the hospital social worker, but yes. We weren't going to allow her to go home with him." She tapped one slender finger against her lips. "I think it was the social worker, but she had already notified CPS."

"How'd Hutton take it?" Morgan asked.

Imani's eyes got wide. "Not well, I'll tell you that much. When he realized what was happening, he started hollering. He was going to sue us all and take our licenses." She sniffed. "As if."

"Did he threaten anything beyond suing?" Morgan asked.

Imani rotated the chair back and forth as she thought. "You mean like physical violence?"

"Exactly like that."

“I think so. I think he got focused on poor Dr. Windham. Said he’d make her life hell. Something like that.” Imani shrugged. “It happens. They generally cool down after a bit.”

Morgan stood. “Thanks, Imani.”

“That’s it?” She seemed surprised.

“For now. Someone else might have questions later.”

She stood, too, one hand braced on the desk. “You think this has something to do with what happened to Dr. Windham?”

Morgan shook his head. “I can’t say. I think it’s something someone should look into, though.”

He knew exactly who that someone should be. He shot off a text to Danielle as he strode out of the Emergency Department. “I have a lead.”

His phone rang before he even got out of the building. “What do you mean by a lead?” she asked without preamble once he answered the phone.

“I mean I found a patient who might have had a grudge against both Lexa and Michelle. A man named Cole Hutton lost custody of his daughter. Lexa had ordered a blood test and Michelle was the lab tech who ran it. His blood alcohol level was high plus he had Fentanyl in his system.”

“And how did you find this out?” she asked, suspicion clear in her voice.

“Asked around.” She didn’t need to know about the extensive file search. “I remembered Lexa talking about the case. It would have been when Michelle was still working at Georgetown.”

Danielle made a noise that didn’t sound like she believed him, but she didn’t question him further. “Give me the man’s name and I’ll check into him. I’ll pick you up at nine.”

CHAPTER THIRTEEN

At 8:57 the next morning, Morgan's door buzzed. He hit the intercom switch. "Yes?"

"I'm downstairs," Danielle said and then cut the connection.

Well, at least she hadn't snuck in to show up at his apartment door this time. He came downstairs to find her double-parked in front of the building. She unlocked the door to the sedan and he climbed in.

"Cole Hutton works at a Giant Food over on 7th Street Northwest." She signaled, glanced over her shoulder, and then pulled smoothly into traffic. "We'll head there first."

Morgan nodded and sat back. He wasn't crazy about being driven some place. He preferred to be the driver, to be in control. At least Danielle didn't have him stomping on an imaginary brake. It used to drive Ashley crazy when he did that and she finally just let him drive.

The rain started falling again. Danielle turned on the wipers. "So who did you speak to when you were asking around?"

"Well, the most important person is a nurse who works in the Emergency Department. She was there the night Hutton was brought in."

The wipers swished a few times. "And she remembers Hutton threatening Lexa in particular?"

"Yes. I guess he started out with the usual. He was going to sue the hospital, but he moved on pretty quickly to focus on Lexa."

Danielle pulled into the grocery store parking lot and selected a parking place in the back row of the lot near the driveway. She strode across the parking lot. Morgan kept pace beside her. "Are we getting our steps in or is there a reason to park as far from the entrance as possible?"

"It's a good spot if we have to leave quickly."

"Do you anticipate that?" Morgan's steps slowed. Once again, that sensation of having gotten himself into an unfamiliar place came over him. The man they were going to talk to could be responsible for two cold-blooded murders. He'd let himself get so caught up in the puzzle of figuring out who might have a grudge against both Lexa and

Michelle that he'd lost sight of the kind of person they were trying to find.

"Hutton wouldn't be the first person to run when the FBI shows up asking questions. It's kind of a thing." Danielle glanced over her shoulder at him and he hurried to catch up.

The doors of the Giant swished open before them and Danielle went up to the information desk. She took her badge off her belt and held it up for the young man behind the desk to see. He was a good-looking kid, probably barely out of high school. He had tousled blond hair and blue eyes and a name tag that read Anthony. His Adam's apple jumped up and down in his long throat and his eyes grew wide as he looked at Danielle's badge.

"I'd like to speak to the manager." She clipped the badge back onto her belt.

"That's, uh, me right now. For this shift." He blushed. Kid didn't look old enough to manage tying his own shoes.

"Great," Danielle said, putting her badge away. "We're looking for an employee of yours. Cole Hutton. Is he here today?"

Anthony turned to the computer next to him and typed a few things in and frowned. "Not today. Looks like he was scheduled for yesterday afternoon and called in sick. Haven't heard from him yet today, but I'm guessing he's still under the weather." He turned back to Danielle. "Can I ask why?"

Danielle ignored his question and asked one of her own. "Does he often call in sick?"

He went back to the computer, but then shook his head. "No. He's pretty reliable."

So either he really was sick or he had a good reason to skip work yesterday and today. Morgan didn't like it one bit. Apparently, Danielle didn't either. "Thanks," she said to the kid and then she was striding so fast out of the grocery store that Morgan thought he might have to jog to keep up.

Back in the car, Danielle punched his a few buttons on her cell phone. Then she said, "Yeah. He wasn't at his place of work. I'm going to check out his residence now." She listened for a moment, then said, "No. I don't think I need back up. We're just chatting."

She hung up and then pulled out of the parking place and out into traffic.

Hutton lived in a sober living home on Hayes Avenue. Morgan had his first prickle of unease. The guy was clearly making an effort. Had he managed to turn his life around? Of course, that wouldn't stop him from blaming Lexa for making him turn his life around in the first place.

From the outside, the house was indistinguishable from most of the other houses on the block. It was a two-story brick home with a porch that ran the length of the front of the house. The rain had started to let up when they arrived, but the sidewalk was still dark with dampness and the air still held the heavy promise of more moisture. Danielle marched up the steps and rang the doorbell. Morgan stood behind her and to one side.

The man who answered the door had gray hair pulled up into a man bun on top of his head and a pair of glasses perched on his nose. His skin was a little darker than Danielle's and he wore jeans and a Henley. "May I help you?"

Danielle showed him her badge. "FBI. We were hoping to talk to Cole Hutton."

The man's eyebrows went up. "He's not here right now. He's at work."

Danielle shook her head. "I'm afraid not."

The man opened the door wider. "You'd better come in."

Once they were inside, he stuck out his hand. "My name's Emilio. I'm the house manager. Is Cole in trouble?"

Danielle shook his hand. "Not yet. We just have a few questions. Any idea where he'd be if he isn't at work?"

Emilio leaned against the wooden banister of the stairway, looking back and forth between Danielle and Morgan. "No. Not really. The clients aren't supposed to hang around the house during the day. We expect them to be out working or looking for work, taking classes. Something." He paused for a second. "Do you want to see his room?"

Danielle took a step back. "We don't have a warrant."

Emilio shrugged. "One of the conditions of living here is that you give up an expectation of privacy. Your room can be searched at any time. We can ask them to do a drug test at any time, too."

Morgan was ready to bound up the stairs to take a look, but Danielle was clearly more reluctant. "We could look from the doorway," he suggested. "Just see if there's anything that could point us to where he might be."

"Okay then." She nodded her assent.

Emilio led them up the stairs to the second floor. There were four bedrooms on that floor. Emilio pulled out a set of keys and led them to the first one on the right. "This is Cole's room." His cell phone rang and he glanced at it. "I need to take this. I'll be right back." He walked down the hall to the stairs.

Morgan stuck his head into the room. It was fairly large. It held a full-sized bed, a bureau with a small television on top of it, a desk, and an arm chair. Nothing was new or all that trendy, but it was clean. The bed was made. A stack of mail sat on the desk next to a neat stack of popsicle sticks. There was a bottle of glue next to that. There was a bulletin board over the desk with notes and photos stuck to it. Morgan squinted from across the room.

Coupons for pizza delivery, a flyer about a special assembly at Sycamore Lane Elementary School, a photo of a little girl. *Okay, Mr. Hutton. You're not here and you're not at work. Where are you?* He looked over at Danielle. "What do you think?"

"I'm not sure, but I'm concerned. I don't like that his whereabouts are unknown." She chewed her lower lip. "We need to find him."

"Do you think he's our guy?" Morgan asked.

She blew out a breath. "I don't think he's not our guy. Not yet. I don't like the idea that he might be out right now stalking his next victim."

Morgan walked over to the desk and ran a finger across one of the popsicle sticks. Why would a grown man have popsicle sticks and school glue out on his desk? The only reason he could think of was that he had those things for his daughter. Maybe for some kind of school project or an arts and crafts afternoon. Nothing had been done with them yet, though. There were no little girl shoes or clothes that he could see. No toys or books. The little girl hadn't been here yet.

But there had been a photo and a flyer. He looked up at the bulletin board. Sycamore Lane Elementary. The assembly was today. Morgan glanced at his watch. It would be starting soon. He unpinned the flyer from the board.

"I think we should go to Hutton's daughter's school." Morgan walked back to the door, holding the flyer.

Danielle frowned at him. "Why?"

"Because I think that's where he might be."

"Same question. Why?"

"Just a feeling. He's got this little craft project all set up, but it doesn't look like his daughter has spent any time here. Maybe it's a bit of wishful thinking. A guy who was wishing he could spend time with his daughter might watch her from afar, if he couldn't actually spend time with her. There's some kind of special assembly today. Lots of parents around. He might be able to blend into the crowd or at least think that he could." In his head, he felt the pieces clicking into place.

"You're basing all that on a stack of popsicle sticks and a bottle of school glue?" Danielle made a face.

"That and what's not here, too." He looked up at the ceiling, trying to gather his thoughts. "Sometimes when you're making a diagnosis, what's not there is just as important as what is there. What symptoms doesn't the patient have? What tests haven't been run? His daughter's not here. I don't think she's ever been here. But there are craft supplies and information about something at her school."

Danielle fisted her hands on her hips and sighed. "Well, it's not like I have any better ideas. Let's go."

CHAPTER FOURTEEN

Sycamore Lane Elementary was only a mile and a half from Hutton's apartment. They drove past it and pulled into a parking place about a block away.

Morgan unzipped his jacket as they walked down the sidewalk toward the school just as Danielle pulled on her suit jacket. He gave her a quizzical look.

"Hides the badge and gun better," she said to Morgan's raised eyebrows. "Don't want to alarm anyone."

A soft breeze, still tinged with rain, blew down the street carrying the scent of cherry blossoms with it. They were miles from the Tidal Basin, but it seemed like all of D.C. smelled like cherry blossoms in the spring. It was a hopeful smell, one that promised sunshine and sweetness.

When was the last time Morgan had allowed either of those things into his life?

The school was a four-story red brick Italianate building with a long set of steps leading up to the entrance. There were quite a few couples making their way down the sidewalks and up the central staircase to the entrance. Morgan and Danielle blended in. Just another set of parents coming to the assembly. He looked around for someone who didn't, someone looking nervous or out of place.

"Tie your shoe," Danielle said under her breath as she stopped on the sidewalk.

He turned to her. "What?" His shoe wasn't untied.

"I said, tie your shoe. Or pretend to. We need a plausible reason to stop here for a moment and my shoes don't have laces."

Ah. He knelt down and untied and retied one of his shoes.

"Do the other one," she said.

He complied. "What are you looking for?"

"Hutton." She swiveled around, scanning the people going up to the school. Her eyes narrowed.

"You see something?" Morgan asked as he stood.

“Maybe.” She nodded her head toward the parking lot. “There’s a guy sitting on the bench over there. Everybody else is hustling in. He’s not moving.”

“Do you think it’s Hutton?” His heart kicked up a notch and his mouth went dry. Were they about to confront Lexa’s killer? Was the man who had tricked her and taken her life sitting on a bench waiting to go into a school to see his daughter get a certificate? Lexa would never get to do something so ordinary and mundane. If Hutton was the murderer, he took all that from Lexa.

Morgan’s hands clenched into fists.

“Maybe. He’s got that hood up. It makes it hard to see his face. Let’s stroll over that way and check him out. Emphasis on stroll. I don’t want to spook him.”

They made their slow way over toward the parking lot, looking pretty much everywhere except at the man on the bench. From inside the school, a chime sounded and an announcement was made. It was hard to make out the exact words, but the gist was the all-school assembly was starting.

The man rose and began walking toward the school, his face fully visible for a moment.

“It’s him,” Danielle said out of the side of her mouth. She changed the angle of how they were walking so they would intercept him, unbuttoning her jacket as they went. She unclipped her badge from her belt and held it up. “Cole Hutton. FBI.”

Hutton looked up. His eyes went wide and then he was sprinting across the grass. Danielle was at his heels. It took Morgan a second to even register what was happening and by that time both Hutton and Danielle were several yards away. As Morgan watched, Hutton increased his lead on Danielle.

They had him. They had their guy. But he was getting away. Morgan was not going to allow that to happen. The man who had murdered Lexa was not going to slip through their fingers. Not today.

Hutton was running down the busy street toward where Danielle had parked. He was going to have to get off it if he was going to completely shake her. His speed was flagging. Hers was staying steady. Still, if he could veer off, he could get away. If Morgan were Hutton, he’d try to get into the park that was a block up. There’d be places to hide in there. Multiple entrances and exits that would allow someone to slip away.

If Morgan could get there first, cut Hutton off, block his escape routes, Danielle would be able to catch him.

Morgan took off like a shot. By angling toward the park on the side streets, he'd be able to get there before Hutton. If anyone thought it was strange to see a man in jeans barreling through their neighborhood in the middle of the day, they didn't do anything about it.

He burst into the park. Nothing but trees and bushes and playground equipment. Had he missed them? He ran toward the area where he thought Hutton would enter. There he was. Breathing hard, but still moving. Danielle was not in sight.

Without thinking, Morgan launched himself through the air and collided with Hutton. They collapsed onto the grass.

"What the hell, man?" Hutton yelled, struggling against Morgan's grasp. "Let me go."

Forget that. "No way. You stay down. " Morgan pinned Hutton to the ground.

"Get off him, Morgan. Get off him right now." Danielle had arrived. She'd only been seconds behind.

Morgan sat back on his heels and brushed the leaves and loose grass off the front of his jacket. He'd got him. He'd kept him from getting away. He'd made sure Hutton was going to pay for what he did. The adrenaline coursing through him was better than any drug he'd ever heard of.

Danielle helped Cole Hutton to his feet, cuffed him, and read him his rights. "Come on, Mr. Hutton. I'd like to have a chat with you." She walked away with him, her hand on his elbow, after shooting Morgan a quick glare over her shoulder.

What was her problem? They got him, didn't they? A thrill of excitement ran through him as he considered that he might have been integral in cracking the case. It was almost as good as making a really tricky diagnosis.

Morgan got to his feet on his own, inspecting the damage he'd done. It wasn't too bad. Some mud. A tear in his shirt near the shoulder. Totally worth it.

They hadn't even gotten back to the school before Hutton started talking. "I just wanted to see my little girl," he protested. "I was going to slip into the assembly right as it started, stay in the back, see her, and slip out before anyone knew I was there. I know I'm not supposed to be on school grounds. I know I'm not allowed to drive her anywhere. I can't believe they'd send the FBI over this! No wonder this country is going to hell in a handbasket."

Danielle stopped and turned to Mr. Hutton. "You think we're here to talk to you about you being on school grounds?"

"You aren't?"

Danielle shook her head. "We'd like to talk to you about Dr. Lexa Windham."

"Who?" If Hutton was acting, he deserved an Oscar for it. Morgan's exhilaration started to turn to unease. "I don't know any Lexa Windham."

Morgan opened his mouth to ask about Michelle Schultz, but Danielle shot him a look so filled with ice that he clammed up and they made the rest of the drive in silence except for Danielle's call to someone at headquarters letting them know they were bringing in a suspect.

Once they were downtown, Danielle pulled into the parking garage attached to the headquarters. Two men emerged from a doorway where they'd clearly been waiting. "Who do you have there, Hernandez?" the taller of the two asked.

Danielle stepped out of the car. "That would be Mr. Cole Hutton. He is a suspect in the deaths of Michelle Schultz and Lexa Windham, but don't book him for those. Let's go for obstruction of justice."

The shorter agent laughed. "He ran?"

She nodded. Morgan got out of the car to stand beside her.

"This guy, too?" the short one asked.

Danielle shook her head this time. "No. This is Morgan Stark. He's consulting on the case."

"Looks like a pretty active consultation." The agent pointed at Morgan's torn shirt and muddy clothes.

"A little too active," Danielle said, striding toward the elevators.

Morgan followed her. "What now?"

"They'll book Hutton and take him to an interview room where I will question him." She glared at him. "You may watch from the observation area, but that's it."

"What if I think of a question you should ask?" What was the big deal?

"Write it down. You can give it to me later." They got off the elevator and Danielle led him to where he could watch the interrogation from. "You need anything? A glass of water? A towel?"

Morgan shook his head.

"Fine. I'll be back. Stay here." She stopped at the doorway to glare at him again. "I mean it. Stay here."

She left Morgan in the observation area and returned a few minutes later with some file folders and a notepad. She went into the interview room and sat with her back toward Morgan. In a minute or two, the two agents led Hutton in and handcuffed him to the table.

"Need anything else, Agent Hernandez?" the tall one asked.

"No. Thanks, Hedley. I appreciate the assist."

"Anytime." The agent left, shutting the door behind him.

"Mr. Hutton, where were you on Wednesday night between ten and midnight?" Danielle asked.

Good. She was getting right to it.

Hutton looked confused. "What? When?"

"Wednesday. Between ten and midnight. Surely you remember where you were, Mr. Hutton. It was only two nights ago."

Hutton's feet were tapping under the table. "Two nights ago?" He looked up at the ceiling, then snapped his fingers. "That was my night at the soup kitchen. Over on Second Street."

Danielle's head tilted a bit. "Anybody who could verify that?"

Hutton sat back. "Rachelle Goodson. She's the pastor there. We worked together until after 11. We stop serving at 10, but there's lots of clean-up to do and prep for the next morning, too. I'm not sure what time I left, but it was pretty late."

"And you were with the pastor the whole time?" Danielle's shoulders slumped a bit.

"She stepped out now and then to talk to someone privately, but there were other people there working. And the clients, of course." Hutton had stopped tapping his toes.

"Names, please."

He listed off five people. Danielle jotted their names down in her notebook as he spoke. When he was done, she looked up from her notes. "Talk to me about Lexa Windham, now."

Hutton threw up his hands. "I don't know who that is or why you're asking me about her."

"Dr. Windham was the doctor in the Emergency Department who ordered the blood test that was the basis of why they took your daughter away from you, Mr. Hutton. Does her name ring a bell now?"

"Oh, her." Hutton looked down at his hands. "I got pretty mouthy that night, I guess."

"You did. You threatened her." Danielle sat back in her chair.

Hutton made a face. "I should apologize to her, try to make amends. In the end, she did me a favor. I'm clean now and working the program to stay that way. If I can keep it up, I'll get visitation rights back and I'll be able to spend time with Ellie again. I had to hit my rock bottom and having them take my little girl away from me that night was it."

Morgan leaned in. Was this guy for real?

"You won't be able to apologize to Dr. Windham. She was murdered two nights ago." Danielle's delivery was deadpan, which only made the impact of her words greater.

Hutton gasped and shoved back from the table. "She was what? Oh, my God. Was she one of those women who worked at hospitals who got killed? And you think I had something to do with it?" He shook his head hard. "No no no no no. I had nothing to do with that. Talk to Pastor Goodson. She'll tell you. I was at the soup kitchen all night. It's part of my Twelve Steps. I'm trying to take what I've learned and bring it forward into the world."

Danielle scratched the side of her neck. "So why'd you run when I approached you, Mr. Hutton?"

He put his head in his hands. "I'm not supposed to be on the school grounds. I can only see Ellie when the visits are supervised and I wanted to see her in that play. She was so proud that she got to play the fox. I helped her memorize her lines. I wanted to be there."

"And you thought the FBI was going to come and arrest you for a visitation violation?" Morgan didn't have to see Danielle's face to know there was a look of disbelief on it. It probably mirrored his own.

Hutton looked up at her. "I didn't think. I reacted. You flashed that badge and that was it."

"Okay, Mr. Hutton. You sit tight. I'm going to have some agents check your alibi. Once we've confirmed that you're not lying to us, we'll cut you loose." She got up and came out of the room. She went into the observation area and shut the door behind her. "He's not our guy."

"You're sure? Maybe his alibi won't check out." They were dropping this guy as a suspect already?

"I doubt it. That was a fairly long list of names. We'll check, but I don't think it's him. Now how about you tell me what the hell you were thinking, Morgan." She sounded angrier at him than she had at Hutton.

It embarrassed him, but he realized that his answer was virtually the same as Hutton's. He hadn't been thinking. "I thought he was going to get away and that I could provide some back up." He crossed his arms over his chest. He wasn't crazy about her tone. She was the one who had asked him to work this case with her, after all.

She drew in a big breath and then let it out. Letting her head lean back against the wall, she closed her eyes. "What if Hutton had actually been our guy and had a knife? He's already killed twice. He's not going to hesitate a third time."

Morgan blanched. He hadn't thought about that. All he'd thought about was catching the guy. "But he was getting away."

"Maybe. Maybe not. I can keep that pace up for a minimum of six or seven miles and he was already gasping for air." Danielle shrugged. "Regardless, he's not a guy with a lot of options. We'd have found him again. Look, I get what you were trying to do and it's my own fault. I asked you to help and I haven't really defined the parameters of what you should and shouldn't do. Can we put tackling suspects on the list of 'shouldn't do,' please?" She straightened.

Morgan nodded his assent. He wasn't sure he meant it though. She had a point. If Hutton had been the killer and had been armed with a knife, he could have gutted Morgan before Danielle got there.

On the other hand, now they knew for sure and wouldn't have to chase him further. Plus, Morgan hadn't felt this way for years. Energized. Enervated. Alive. Purpose-driven. He was going to help them find Lexa's killer and put the bastard away forever.

After that? He wasn't sure. He had this to hang onto for now, though. This would keep him going. "What now?"

"Back to the drawing board," Danielle said.

CHAPTER FIFTEEN

Brianna Olson hurried to her car. It took her a second to find it. It was one gray car in a sea of them and sometimes she had to check the license plate before she was sure it was hers.

Sure enough, as she pulled out of the parking lot of Georgetown University Hospital, there was another gray sedan right behind her. She flipped on the radio and tapped her fingers to the beat of the song. She liked this one. It made her think about getting dressed up to go out. Fun. Maybe this weekend. She'd call some girlfriends and they'd go dancing. Assuming she wasn't too tired. Nursing was hard!

The light ahead of her changed and she rolled to a stop. Was that the same car following her that had pulled out of the Georgetown lot behind her? She didn't remember anybody on her shift that would take the exact same route home as her. It was a big hospital, though.

The light turned green and she started up again. The gray car staying right on her tail. She started to feel uneasy. Everyone at the hospital was talking about what had happened to Dr. Windham and then there was that lab tech that had gotten killed, too. Was she being paranoid?

At the next intersection, Brianna turned right without signaling. Damn it. The other car did, too. It didn't mean anything, though. She made two left turns, one right after the other, heading back to the street she'd been on.

The gray car was still there.

Damn it all to hell. Fine. She'd give whoever this was a run for his money. She'd grown up here. She knew her way around. She'd take the scenic way home and lose whoever this clown was on the way. She headed west toward Woolsey where she grew up. No way would he be able to keep up with her on those windy twisty roads.

He definitely was struggling. A couple of times, Brianna thought she'd lost him only to have him turn up in her rear view mirror a few minutes later.

She accelerated as she hit a particularly winding stretch. When she was in high school, she and her friends used to come out here to drink and smoke. There were houses nearby. Big ones. But they were far back from the road and there were plenty of turnouts where a bunch of kids could meet. She'd driven this road when she most definitely should not have been behind a wheel.

She was stone cold sober now. She took the S curve like Danica Patrick. "Wheee!" It was kind of exhilarating.

She glanced in the rearview mirror. The gray car hadn't made the turn. It was off the road, its nose in a ditch. Served the bastard right.

She made a U-turn to head back home. He wasn't going to be following her now. A twinge of guilt ran through her. She'd only wanted him to stop following her. She hadn't wanted to hurt him.

She slowed as she made her way past the car. It was still light out. She could see the figure behind the wheel. It was slumped forward. Had he been injured? Was he even conscious? It was pretty isolated out here. Cell service was spotty. Who knew how long it would be before someone came along to help him? And if that person would be able to summon help?

She stopped and made another U-turn, pulling over to the side of the road. She got out of her car. "Are you okay?" she yelled.

No answer. Not even a twitch in the slumped figure.

She walked closer. "Hey! You! Are you hurt?"

She was close enough to look inside the car now. It was a man and he was completely slumped against the wheel, eyes closed. Was he hurt?

Okay. So the guy had it coming. Who follows someone like that? But she wasn't going to be able to live with herself if she didn't make sure he was okay.

She knocked on the window. Nothing. No response.

She tried the door. Surprisingly, it was unlocked. "Are you okay? Do you need help?" She leaned in to shake him by the shoulder.

Suddenly he had her arm. His grip was so strong. She couldn't pull back. "What are you doing?"

"I'm making sure you pay for what you did, Brianna."

And then she saw the knife.

CHAPTER SIXTEEN

Morgan looked out the window of the conference room. The sun lowered in the sky. Trees cast long shadows across the sidewalk. All the adrenaline rush of bringing Cole Hutton in had fled his system.

Danielle sat on the edge of the conference room table, gazing at the boards, as if something there might jump out at her. "There has to be something more, something more specific that connects these two. Hutton was the only case where Lexa was in charge and Michelle did the lab work. So what else is there? Do they go to the same gym? Shop at the same grocery store? Belong to the same club?"

Morgan walked over to perch next to her. "I can't find anything like that in these files. We've been over them three times already. We need more information, something that will help us see what the pattern is."

Danielle's phone buzzed and she pulled it out of her pocket. "Hernandez."

She stood straight up. "Where?" She grabbed a piece of paper and wrote down an address. "We're on our way."

"On our way where?" Morgan asked after she'd hung up.

"I think we're about to get more information. There's a third victim."

***

Morgan stood out of the way and watched as the crime scene investigators crawled over the area, taking samples and marking locations. The light was fading fast, and a sense of urgency buzzed through the atmosphere.

Another set of techs were working on Brianna Olson's car where it sat on the other side of the road, headlights still on, driver's side door open, keys still in the ignition.

Whatever the reason she'd had for getting out of her car, she hadn't intended on being gone long.

The car had been what prompted the older gentleman who had called in the situation to stop in the first place. He'd seen the car pulled over on the side of the road and had slowed to see if someone was in trouble and needed help. He'd probably expected to help someone change a tire or call for help. Instead, he'd seen Brianna's body on the opposite side of the road and had realized that she needed much more than he could offer.

Brianna's body was now mercifully covered with a sheet, but Morgan had seen her up close before they'd covered her. He recognized her. He'd seen her around the hospital and he thought she might have been the nurse on one or more of his cases. He probably wouldn't have been able to come up with her name if he'd been asked. He zipped his jacket against the chill that had come into the air.

The poor girl was splayed on the side of the road as if she was a piece of garbage someone had tossed out a window. Images of Lexa's body by the Dumpster filled his brain. Was that part of this madman's message? Was he somehow implying these women were trash?

Whoever he was, he couldn't be farther from the truth.

And why was Brianna's body so far from her car? What had persuaded her to get out and cross this road?

If it was the same person as the one who had killed Lexa and Michelle – the unsub, as Danielle referred to him – the answer was obvious. He'd somehow convinced Brianna that he needed help. What had he done? Pulled to the side of the road? Made it look like he'd been in an accident? Or had a medical emergency? Damn this man. It enraged Morgan that this monster was playing on the best and kindest instincts these women had to lure them to him. The murderer knew that Brianna and Michelle and Lexa would stop to help a total stranger. He understood their empathy and compassion. Then he used it against them.

Twilight was approaching. Morgan walked up the road to try to get his emotions under control and to see if there was anything interesting in that direction before the light failed. There wasn't a lot he could do while the crime scene investigators were still working. Danielle had gone to be part of the group that was talking to people in the few houses along this road. Chances of them having heard anything weren't good, but they had to cover every base. What was Brianna doing out here anyway? He'd be surprised if she lived any place nearby. It all felt so futile. He kicked a pine cone in front of him as he went.

Then he stopped. In front of him, there were clear marks of someone having made a rapid U turn in the road. He looked down the road toward the crime scene. Brianna would have been able to see that spot in her rearview mirror. Had something happened that made her turn around to look? Maybe the sound of another car crashing?

Morgan jogged back down the road and waved over one of the crime scene investigators, a young Black man with glasses. “I’m not sure this means anything, but there are some tire marks in the road up there.” He pointed to where he’d walked.

The man squinted up the road. “Tire marks?”

“Like someone made a fast U-turn.”

“I’ll take a look. If they’re a match for the car, it could be helpful.” He made a note on his clipboard and started to walk away.

“Finding anything else that looks interesting?” Morgan asked.

The investigator glanced over his shoulder to see if anyone was listening and then said, “No. Not a thing. We’ll maybe be able to get an idea of his vehicle from the tire tracks, but it’s a real long shot.”

It felt like the whole thing was a long shot. They were searching for the connection, but without knowing what form it would take, it was hard to figure out where to look.

In the hospital, Morgan generally knew where to look. He could see the signs of what was off, what wasn’t quite right. Out here with Danielle, everything was new. He felt off kilter, unmoored.

More than that, though, he felt rage. Who was this man who felt he had the right to cut short these lives? People often accused doctors of playing God. They had a point. Doctors made life and death decisions every day, but not like this. This was pure evil.

And Morgan was going to seek out the root of it and destroy it before it could destroy anyone else. They’d been too late to save Brianna Olson. He wasn’t going to let that happen again.

CHAPTER SEVENTEEN

An hour later, Morgan was back in Danielle's FBI vehicle, and they were headed back into the city without much of a feeling of accomplishment. Beyond the tire tracks, he hadn't contributed much. Or, at least, it felt that way.

"I don't see how Brianna is connected to Lexa or to Michelle," he said. He adjusted the shoulder harness of the seat belt. "Except for the obvious and that doesn't seem like enough."

What would be enough to take someone's life? What kind of person plotted and planned to end someone else's existence? Morgan didn't understand it.

He spent nearly every waking minute of every day trying to save as many lives as he could. He started and ended each day looking for ways to relieve suffering and extend lives. Most days, he managed to do that for at least one person. For years, that was what had driven him forward, through medical school and his sister's disappearance and his parents' deaths. He'd found purpose in helping others.

When had that stopped being enough? When had those triumphs ceased to spring him out of bed every day? When had he become so weary?

He spread his hands out in front of himself and looked at them. He hadn't done any of those things today. He hadn't prescribed a medication, requested a test, or performed a procedure that would help anyone. He had, however, felt every bit as driven as he ever had in the hospital. He would stop this murderer from taking another life.

"The connection's there. We'll find it." Danielle pulled off 695 on the exit that would take them to Morgan's apartment.

He envied her confidence. "Whoa," he said. "Where are we going?"

"I'm taking you home and then I'm going to go get some sleep myself." She steered the car through the darkened streets.

"But we need to start looking at Brianna's case. We need to see if somehow she'll make the connection between all three of them clearer. Let's keep going." He doubted he'd be able to sleep anyway. He was too keyed up.

Danielle shook her head. "Nope, Dr. Stark. It's time to call it a day. We'll pick it up again tomorrow when we're fresher. Besides, we won't have anything from the crime scene unit until then."

"We should look at what we've got so far," Morgan argued.

Danielle made another turn and pulled up in front of Morgan's apartment building. "Tomorrow. Do you want me to pick you up?"

Morgan knew when he was beat. "Sure."

He got out of the car and watched it until it turned the corner out of sight.

He looked up at his building and a heaviness returned to his heart. He'd spent the day with his brain and his body fully engaged in something. Now what? The recliner chair and a delivery pizza?

It hardly seemed worth it.

He collected his mail – junk mail and bills – and trudged up the stairs. He took a quick shower to wash off the last of the mud that still clung to him from tackling Cole Hutton in the park and took up his position in the recliner chair, glass of Scotch in hand.

He flicked on the news.

It was surreal. The reporter – a pretty Asian-American woman with dark hair blowing around her face – was standing exactly where Morgan had been standing not more than an hour ago. The winding road disappeared behind her, but you could still see the crime scene unit finishing up on the side of the road, harsh temporary lights glaring down on them.

"The body of a young woman was discovered in this remote area late this afternoon. Police have yet to release any information on the victim's name, pending notification of the family. WLVX-TV has been hearing that the victim is another health care worker. No word on whether this crime is linked to the murders of Lexa Windham and Michelle Schultz."

The screen switched to a generic background with photos of Lexa and Michelle, side by side, on top of it.

Morgan slumped back into his chair. Lexa. Maybe that was why he'd been keen to keep going. Here, back in his apartment, alone with his thoughts, the reasons why he was involved in this investigation came crashing back in.

Danielle might want him there for his eye for detail and his unique way of putting information together. He wanted to be there because he wanted to get the son-of-a-bitch who had cut short such a promising young life. He drained the Scotch in one swallow.

They'd never caught the man who'd taken Fiona. They'd never even found her body. It had left an open wound in Morgan's heart and it had killed their parents. His father had died of a heart attack the following year and two years after that his mother had succumbed to cancer. On the surface, it was all unrelated. As a doctor who tried to look at the whole patient, he was way too aware that there was more to it than that. He was convinced his father had died of a broken heart and that his mother had let grief poison her very blood.

What was he doing here? What was the point of any of it?

He felt empty inside. He needed contact with someone. He fished his phone out of his pocket and let his finger hover the button that would call Ashley.

He let his hand drop. No. He wouldn't make matters worse by burdening Ashley with his existential crisis.

He'd already made her life difficult enough. Christ, he hadn't gotten those papers notarized yet, either. Maybe tomorrow.

When Fiona had disappeared, he had thrown himself into his career. He'd been driven before. People don't get into medical school and persevere through the grueling training without having drive and ambition. He'd kicked it up to a whole new level then and that was how he'd led his life since.

Lexa's murder was hitting him in much the same way as Fiona's disappearance had. He felt that same emptiness inside, the same questioning of what his purpose was, the same despair. Throwing himself into his work no longer seemed like the answer, though.

CHAPTER EIGHTEEN

It's dark. A rattling sound behind him makes Morgan whirl. Nothing is behind him, though. Just an empty street. The wind chases loose leaves down the alley, their path leaving a slight scent of decay behind them. The Dumpster is ahead of him on his left. Lexa's feet peek out from behind the rusted metal, a startling bit of color in the grayed out moonlight he's navigating by.

He races to her. A sheet already covers most of her body. He whips it off her face and leaps back, gasping. It's not Lexa. It's Fiona, lying broken and bleeding behind the Dumpster.

A siren sounds startling him.

Morgan sat up, heart pounding, sweat coating his body. He wasn't in an alley behind a Dumpster. He was in his apartment, in his own bed, and there was no siren. Just his phone ringing.

Ashley.

He sighed. He should let her find him a damn notary. They'd both be happier in the end. He picked up the phone. "Sorry," he said.

There was a moment of silence. "I accept your apology, but I want to be sure you know what you're apologizing for." That was Ashley. She liked her i's dotted and her t's crossed.

"I haven't had a chance to get those papers notarized." He pinched the bridge of his nose. He would get to it today, one way or the other. He would make it a priority.

"No. You haven't. But that's not what this is about. This isn't a personal call."

Morgan sat up a little straighter in bed, the sheet puddling at his waist. "Okay."

"Morgan, were you using your privileges here at Georgetown to look through multiple patients' charts? Patients that weren't yours?"

Oh. That's what this was about. The snooping through Lexa's cases looking for a connection with Michelle. Georgetown University granted Morgan permission to admit and treat patients. That's what his privileges were. It didn't give him carte blanche to maraud through files. He'd known that when he'd done it. He'd been convinced that it was the key to finding Lexa's killer and stopping whatever twisted spree he was on. Instead, it hadn't gotten them anywhere. It certainly hadn't helped Brianna. How had he gotten busted so fast? "How do you know that?"

"That's hardly relevant, Morgan."

She was right. He sighed. "All right. What is relevant?"

"What's relevant is that not only did you access patients' private information without their consent, you then shared that information with the FBI. It's a huge breach of trust, Morgan. You know that. If people think we're going to be turning their personal information over to law enforcement without officials so much as even getting a warrant or a subpoena, they won't seek health care. We're talking here about our most vulnerable, too." She was building up a head of steam. She wasn't wrong, though.

"You're right. I'm sorry. I . . . I just wanted to figure out what happened to Lexa and to Michelle. Really, my main goal was to protect others. It's possible Brianna's death is linked as well. Who knows when this person is going to stop? How many more he might kill if we don't find him and stop him?" She needed to understand that while his methods might have been questionable, his motives were not.

There was silence on the other end. He'd taken the wind out of her sails with an argument he knew she'd have trouble countering. Preventing someone from coming to harm? That was one hundred percent Ashley's goal in life. "The young woman on the news last night? She was one of ours?"

Morgan rubbed his forehead. Probably shouldn't have let that particular cat out of the bag. "Yes, but it's not public knowledge yet. They have to notify the family."

"What's going on here, Morgan? Do you think someone is targeting people on the Georgetown University Hospital staff?" A note of fear had crept into her voice.

"I do." He hadn't wanted to frighten her. That hadn't been his intention. Maybe a little fear was a good thing, though. Maybe she'd be a little more careful and maybe she'd understand a little bit better why he had so seriously violated protocol.

She sighed. "Okay, Morgan. I get it. I do. It can't happen again, though."

"Absolutely not."

"I'm serious, Morgan. I think I'll be able to cover for you this time, but I won't be able to do it a second time. I'm not willing to lose my job over this even if you're willing to risk your job and your license."

He started. His license? Surely, it wouldn't go that far.

"And I think you should extend your leave of absence. I think it might be better if no one saw your face around here for a week or two."

"Heard and understood," he said.

"Okay. I'm going to go to try to clean this mess up as best as I can."

"Thanks, Ash."

"I'm sending you a list of notaries nearby, too, Morgan. Please sign the papers and return them."

Morgan rested his forehead on his drawn-up knees. "I will."

"Thanks, Morgan." She paused, but didn't hang up. He could hear her breathing. "And Morgan? Take care of yourself please. I know how you can get. Be careful."

He was about to open his mouth and say that he had an FBI agent practically attached to his hip so he was pretty well protected, but he knew that wasn't precisely what she meant. "I'll do my best, Ash. I really want to help solve this, though. It's got something to do with the hospital. I know it."

She made a little noise in the back of her throat. "It's not like your motives are ever bad, Morgan. I know that. Anyone who has worked with you knows that. You sometimes go too far, though. You push the envelope until it bursts."

It touched him that she still cared. "I'll be careful," he promised.

"See that you are, Morgan." Then she was gone.

Morgan set the phone down next to him. Outside, the day was gray. The rain had returned. There was a flash of light, followed a few seconds later by huge boom. Great. A thunderstorm. He hoped they got every shred of evidence there was at Brianna's crime scene. If they hadn't, whatever was left would be washed away.

He fell back against the pillows. How much worse could it get?

A hell of a lot worse. If someone besides Ashley had figured out that he had gone through patient records and shared sensitive information with the FBI, he could lose his license, whether it was for a good reason or not. Then where would he be? Who would he be?

His job hadn't been giving him the satisfaction it had for years. It wasn't enough anymore, but to lose it? To never be able to practice medicine again? To face the world with all that stripped away? He couldn't begin to imagine it. Even the idea made him shudder.

He got out of bed and put coffee and hot water into a French press and went to wash up while it steeped. He stood in the shower, letting the water pound down on him to wash away that nightmare and the thought of the shame he'd feel if he was no longer a doctor.

Dressed and sipping his coffee, he wondered what more he'd have to offer Danielle.

He was a doctor. That's what he knew. That's what he was. Not an FBI agent.

Then it hit him. How would he feel if someone threatened his ability to be a doctor? It was bad enough that he'd done it to himself. What if he was the kind of person who never took responsibility for their actions? Always found a way to blame other people? And someone did something that threatened that very notion of who he was as a person in the world? How viciously might that person fight back?

Would he be willing to kill?

CHAPTER NINETEEN

Danielle took a sip of coffee from her travel mug and put it back into the cupholder as she pulled up in front of Morgan's apartment building and texted him that she was waiting. The building wasn't exactly a dump, but it definitely wasn't what she'd imagined a successful doctor living in. Then she'd heard about his impending divorce and how his wife was selling the fancy McMansion they'd been living in out in Arlington. That made a little more sense.

Only a little, though.

He could afford better. She was reasonably sure of that. It was almost as if he was punishing himself for something.

Morgan wasn't what she'd imagined a successful doctor to be either. He definitely was cocky, but there was more going on there. He truly was mourning the loss of his resident. Danielle's immediate assumption had been there'd been something more going on there than a mentor/student relationship, but if there was, absolutely nobody seemed to know anything about it. Nobody had seen anything untoward and there'd been no evidence of an affair in any of Lexa's belongings.

Morgan came hustling out of the building. She hit the button to unlock the door. He stepped in, smelling of coffee and shampoo. "Morning," she said.

"I had a thought." He buckled his seat belt.

"About what?" she asked, putting the car into drive. She bit back an inward sigh. One of the perks of being an FBI agent was having a car assigned to you. She missed her own ride, though. She liked the feeling she got from driving a manual transmission, feeling like she was one with the car as the gears shifted. This thing was like a boat.

"Maybe we were going at this from the wrong direction. Maybe it's not a patient who's angry at members of the staff. Maybe it's a colleague." His excitement palpable, he turned to look at her

"You mean a doctor or a nurse?" Didn't they all take that 'do no harm' oath? Wouldn't that preclude murdering coworkers?

"Exactly like a doctor or a nurse. Someone who spent a lot of time and money getting through school to get a degree and jumped through all the hoops to get licensed and then—" His words trailed off and he shuddered.

Clearly whatever he had envisioned created a visceral reaction. "And then what?"

"And then did something to get that license revoked or privileges taken away. It would be an incredible blow. There would be shame and embarrassment, loss of income, and . . . loss of their sense of self. Think about it. So much of our identity is caught up in what we do for a living. For a lot of us, it's who we are." He looked down at his hands in his lap.

There was something more going on there, but she didn't have time to pursue it. Danielle changed lanes to get on the highway. She understood what he was saying, though. She couldn't imagine having to stop being an FBI agent, especially if she was being stripped of her badge for misconduct of some kind. "Okay."

"So what if that person was the type who never took responsibility for their own mistakes? You know the kind. It's always someone else's fault or something that was out of their control." His voice dripped with disgust. He clearly didn't have patience for that type.

She definitely understood where he was coming from. The FBI wasn't exactly full of people who were humble and happy to admit any kind of wrongdoing. They were not her favorite co-workers.

"What might a person like that do? Maybe try to get revenge against the people he felt wronged him?" Morgan continued. "Would they go so far as to kill people they thought were responsible? Someone in the medical field would definitely know how to fake an injury convincingly enough to lure someone to them."

It wasn't a bad theory and it was definitely another place to start digging and they needed that. "Do you have anybody specific in mind?"

He turned back to face forward. "No."

"How many people work for the hospital?" Danielle asked.

Morgan shrugged. "If you include everyone – doctors, nurses, techs, physician's assistants, staff – probably around 9,000 people."

Danielle whistled. That was a lot of personnel to look through. "Not a small group. Do you have an idea of how to narrow that down?"

"No, but I've got an idea of who I can ask."

***

Morgan knocked on Ashley's open door on the seventh floor of the hospital's east wing. This part of the hospital looked like any other office building with a large central area for cubicle workers and offices around the perimeter. She looked up from the papers on her desk at his knock. Damn, she was beautiful. It had been close to a decade since he'd first seen her across the room at a hospital function and she still took his breath away. Some silver had started to find its way into her blonde hair and there were some wrinkles beside her eyes that hadn't been there before, but he thought those things only made her more beautiful.

"Morgan, what are you doing here?" Unsaid, but implied in her question, was the fact that she'd suggested he make himself scarce for a while and as usual he wasn't going with the program.

He slipped into her office and pulled the door shut behind him for a little more privacy. "I stopped by to drop off these." He held up a sheaf of papers. He'd actually managed to get them notarized. It hadn't been that difficult and he felt a pang of guilt over how long it had taken him to take care of the errand. She asked so little of him, both in their marriage and now. He should have done more when he had the chance.

She tilted her head to one side and regarded him with those bright blue eyes. "You could have put those in the mail, Morgan. I didn't need you to deliver them personally."

"I thought I'd say hello, too."

She snorted. "Sure you did. You didn't even do that when were married unless you wanted something. So what is it? What do you want?"

He sat down in the chair across from her and looked down at his hands in his lap. Was that true? Had he only stopped by to see his wife when he wanted something from her? God, he'd been such a tool. No wonder she'd left him. "I'm working with the FBI as a consultant," he said.

Setting down the pen she held, she nodded. "And you think I can help somehow?"

"I do, Ash. I have a theory. I think whoever is targeting people might be someone who worked here at the hospital and doesn't anymore. Someone who was forced to leave for some reason and is angry at the people he thinks are responsible." It made so much sense. The person would understand hospital shifts so he'd have an inkling of when people would be coming and going as well as medical knowledge.

She leaned back in her chair and crossed her arms over her chest. "Okay. I see how you got there. It feels pretty extreme, though."

"As extreme as three dead women?" Morgan countered.

She held up her hand to stop him. "Don't. I don't want to be guilted into doing something I shouldn't here and I'm pretty sure you're about to ask me to do exactly that."

She wasn't wrong. He wasn't sure how he felt about her being able to see through him so easily, either. Perhaps he wasn't as slick as he thought. Maybe he'd never been. "How hard would it be to get a list of people who were fired or forced to resign from the hospital in the past six months or so?"

"For me? Not all that hard. For me to tell you? Impossible."

"Why?"

"Because I could lose my job for leaking people's personal information." She rubbed at her chin. "Not many of them fall into the category you're interested in, though. For most people who leave or are let go, this is just a job. You're describing someone for whom this is much more than that. You're looking for someone whose identity and sense of self-worth are tied up in their job. Someone who's invested a lot of time and money in reaching a certain position."

Morgan sat back in his chair. She was so smart. She'd gotten exactly what he was trying to imply. "How does that help me?"

She opened a file drawer behind her and pulled out a stapled sheaf of papers. She slid them across the desk to Morgan. "This is a directory of doctors who had privileges at Georgetown six months ago. These are all the doctors who were able to treat or admit patients here."

"And?" He stared at the pages, not sure what to do with them.

"And you could go through it and see if there's anyone on that list who isn't here anymore. That would give you a narrower list."

"Okay." He took the sheaf of papers and started to leaf through it. He saw her logic. It would be time-consuming, but not impossible. He'd take this list and see if any of those doctors were no longer working at Georgetown. That would give him a shorter list to work with. "Thanks, Ash."

She narrowed her eyes and sighed before she spoke again. "One more thing, but you did not hear it from me. There's one person who will be on that list who was asked to leave because of a pattern of harassing female staff."

“Were Lexa, Brianna, or Michelle victims of the harassment?” He sat back in his chair. Was that the connection they were looking for? It would hardly be in the files the FBI had.

Ashley shook her head. “I can’t share who specifically reported him, but it does seem to fit with what kind of people are getting hurt here. They’ve all been young women, right?”

He nodded.

“The person I’m thinking of doesn’t know who reported him either. He could be making assumptions.”

Morgan stood. “Ashley, thank you so much. I really appreciate it.”

He wanted to cross behind her desk and give her a hug, but he also wanted to respect her space. Maybe if he’d thought a little bit more about what Ashley did or didn’t want, it wouldn’t be so awkward now. He hated that it had taken this long to see his own behavior in this new light. He’d been too caught up in his work and his patients’ needs to step back and take a good long look at himself.

“Don’t mention it.” She waved him off. “Seriously, really don’t mention it. I could get in a lot of trouble for having told you that much. Now go. I have work to do.”

Morgan let himself out of her office, the sheaf of papers nearly burning in his hands. The answer was in there. He could feel it. No way was he going to waste time going home before he dug into the information.

He hurried to his office, waving to the receptionist at the desk in the waiting room as he rushed through. Once there, he shut the door behind himself.

Settling himself behind his desk, he booted up the computer and laid the papers out. Some names he could cross off his list automatically. Ayres, for example. He was still here. Morgan also crossed off all of the female doctors. Most of the names were familiar and he moved through the list quickly as he crossed off anyone that he’d worked with recently as well.

There were a few names that either didn’t ring a bell or were people he hadn’t seen in a while. Those he searched for on the computer. Most of them still worked at Georgetown. There were two that had taken positions at other hospitals. He put question marks by those names in case they hadn’t relocated voluntarily.

There were three doctors who had retired. All three of them were in their seventies and he doubted they would have the physical strength to do what their unsub had done.

Then he hit a name he recognized, but not in a good way. Ward Dolan. Morgan hadn't had to work with him often, but every time he did he walked away annoyed. The guy was condescending and entitled. He wasn't a bad doc, but he rubbed Morgan the wrong way pretty much every time they crossed paths.

Come to think of it, one of those times had been because of an off-color remark Dolan had made about a patient's breasts. Morgan had been so shocked, he hadn't said anything.

He typed Dolan's name in to the computer. He no longer appeared on the Georgetown University list of attending physicians. Then Morgan tried a general search. It didn't look like Dolan had moved to another hospital, either.

He pulled out his phone and texted Danielle. *I've got a lead.*

She texted back. *I'll pick you up in twenty.*

CHAPTER TWENTY

Morgan barely waited for Danielle to stop the car before getting in. She seemed nearly as anxious, not even bothering with saying hello and pulling back onto the road as Morgan buckled his seatbelt. "Tell me again how you zeroed in on this particular guy? What was his name again?"

"Ward Dolan. He left Georgetown abruptly three months ago. No doctor lined up to take his place, no explanation and he doesn't appear to have gone to a different hospital. That's not typical. There's usually a story behind something like that. He still has his license, though, so I doubt the issue was medical malpractice."

"So what do you think it was?"

"It points to more of a personnel issue. I . . . heard a rumor that he may have been harassing female staff members." He didn't want to bring Ashley's name up, even with Danielle. The less involvement she had, the better. "His time at Georgetown overlapped all three of our victims, all of whom were young attractive women."

"Did Lexa ever say anything to you about being harassed?"

Morgan shook his head. "No. But she might not have felt it necessary. If she took it up with Human Resources and they dealt with it, I might never have heard anything about it." He could see Lexa not wanting to share that kind of information with him.

"Do you know for certain which women complained about Dolan?"

Another headshake. "Sorry. No."

Danielle shrugged. "Don't be sorry. I'm just making sure I understand what we're dealing with here. What you're saying is that we have a disgruntled doc here, but there's no direct connection with his disgruntlement and our three victims."

"But there could be," Morgan added. There had to be. It made perfect sense.

"Do you know him? Have you worked with him?" she asked.

"A little. I don't know him well and what I do know I didn't like much." The guy was a pompous ass.

Danielle glanced over at him. "Did he seem prone to violence to you?"

Dolan had never seemed the type to throw a punch. He was more the type of guy who would do something behind your back. "No. Not really."

"You never know what's going to make someone snap," Danielle observed as she pulled up in front of a house with a For Sale sign in the overgrown yard. Morgan stepped out of the vehicle. After so many days of rain, the sun was out and a soft warm breeze made the sign sway. Maybe Morgan had it wrong. Maybe Dolan had taken a position elsewhere and was taking a little time between positions to move. The place looked deserted.

"Somebody apparently isn't concerned about curb appeal." Danielle had gotten out and stood next to him, looking over the property with a bit of disapproval.

It did seem odd. The rest of the neighborhood sported manicured lawns with well-tended flowerbeds. Dolan's place was a mess.

They walked up the sidewalk, stopping to pick up two days' worth of newspapers. Morgan rang the bell, hearing it echo inside the house. No one came to the door. He rang again. The bell worked. He could clearly hear it chiming away, but nothing else. No movement. "Maybe he's not home."

"He's home." Danielle knocked hard, three times on the door just like she'd knocked on his door the other night when he'd tried to ignore her. Had that only been two days ago? "Ward Dolan," she barked. "FBI. Open the door, please."

That got a response. Through the long narrow windows beside the door, Morgan saw a man come into the entryway. The door flew open. "FB-what?"

If Morgan hadn't known they were at Dolan's house, he wouldn't have recognized him. The man he remembered from those encounters had been expensively dressed, carefully manicured, a bit of a peacock.

This guy . . . this guy was a slob. Unshaven, wearing sweatpants that seemed to have doubled as a napkin. His skin was a pasty white as if he hadn't been outside in days and his hair clung greasily to his head. Morgan could smell the booze on the man's breath from across the threshold.

"FBI," Danielle repeated. "May we come in, Dr. Dolan? We'd like to ask you some questions about Michelle Schultz, Lexa Windham, and Brianna Olson."

Dolan took a stumbling step backward as Danielle entered the house. Morgan followed and stopped in the entry way. Something was very wrong here.

A single lamp stood in the sunken living room, its cord trailing across the floor, not plugged into an outlet. There was no other furniture. Two boxes sat side by side, flaps open.

"Stark?" Dolan said. "What the hell are you doing here? Did your bitch wife send you?"

Morgan rounded on him. "Excuse me?"

Dolan leaned forward, enunciating in the way only the very drunk can manage. "I asked if your bitch wife sent you."

Morgan took a step toward him, but Danielle grabbed his arm. She might be slight, but her grip was like iron. He looked down at her and she gave him a quick head shake. He sucked in a breath. Fine. He'd let her ask some questions, but he was not leaving here without making sure Dolan regretted talking about Ashley like that.

"Is there some place we can sit down to talk?" Danielle asked.

Dolan shrugged and ambled off to the right. They walked through a door into a beautiful chef's kitchen that had not been treated kindly lately. The counter was stacked with empty take-out containers and beer bottles. Nobody had cooked here in quite a while. "Sorry," Dolan said as he walked through. "Got a little behind on the housekeeping now that the wife's gone." The whole place smelled like rotting food.

The kitchen opened onto a family room. Dolan plopped down into a recliner chair and picked up the glass of Scotch that sat on the end table next to it. Danielle sat down on the couch across from him. Morgan sat next to her.

Dolan kicked back in the recliner and looked across at them with blood-shot eyes. "Who did you want to talk to me about?"

Danielle listed the names again. Dolan showed no sign of recognition. "I don't know who those people are. Why do you want to talk to me about them?"

"They're all young women who have worked at Georgetown University Hospital that have been murdered in the last week." Danielle's tone was flat, but Morgan could hear the anger in it.

Dolan cocked his head to one side and squinted. "And?"

"And we were wondering, do you have anything you'd like to tell us about your relationships with them?" Danielle asked.

Dolan waved her words away. "Relationships? I have no idea what you're talking about. Didn't even recognize the names."

“How about their faces?” Danielle pulled a set of three photographs out of her jacket and spread them on the coffee table in front of Dolan.

He glanced at them for a second and shook his head immediately. “Nope. No clue.”

Morgan couldn’t take it anymore. He stood up. “Did you kill these women? Did you sexually harass them and then when they reported you to HR and you lost your job, did you decide to take revenge by killing them?”

Dolan stared up at Morgan, a smirk playing at the corner of his mouth. “I have no idea what you’re talking about.”

“I’m talking about you being let go from the hospital for harassing female staff members, Dolan. Do you remember that?” Morgan wanted to wring the man’s neck.

Dolan snapped the footrest of the recliner down and lurched to his feet. “Is that what your wife told you?”

“She didn’t have to, Dolan. Your reputation is all over the hospital.” Morgan didn’t know that for sure, but it was a good guess. He’d heard whispers between female staff members about who to stay away from even if he’d never heard Dolan’s name mentioned specifically.

“Stupid bitches ruined my reputation. None of ‘em can take a joke or a compliment. And when it all hits the fan, the hospital doesn’t have my back. Oh, no. It’s all about zero tolerance. And what am I supposed to do now? Any place I apply to for privileges wants to know why I left Georgetown. What am I supposed to tell them? And, of course, my wife leaves. Apparently, I was basically a wallet. Once I couldn’t support her in the style she had become accustomed to, she was out the door.” He’d taken the few steps needed to be toe to toe with Morgan.

Morgan stood his ground. Dolan had a few pounds on him, but Morgan was pretty sure he could take him. “So what exactly did you joke with those bitches about? What kind of compliment did you pay to Lexa that made her report you to HR and get your ass fired?” Morgan stepped forward.

Dolan took a lurching step backward. “Lexa?” He looked confused for moment, then realization dawned. “Oh, you mean your little side piece? I figured you had dibs. I never touched her.”

“My what?” What had this Neanderthal called Lexa?

“Side piece, Stark. Your little bit of ass on the side. Everyone knows your wife ditched you. Rumor is you hardly ever leave the hospital. I figured you must have been dipping your wick somewhere.

That Brianna was a nice piece of ass, too. Were you boning her, too, Stark? Must be nice to have two in the hand and in the bush, if you know what I mean." The smirk got bigger.

"You sorry excuse for human being. No wonder you were fired. You're disgusting." Morgan took yet another step forward.

"Me? I'm disgusting? I'm not the one parading all over the hospital talking about how special I am, how my skills are so much better than someone else's. That's you, my friend." On the word friend, Dolan poked Morgan with his index finger

Morgan had been expecting something of the sort, though. Dolan was the kind of drunk that would push and shove if he thought he could get away with it. Well, he could forget that. Morgan sidestepped and Dolan crashed forward, tripping over the coffee table and only righting himself at the last minute. "I am not your friend and Lexa wasn't anybody's side piece. She was a young woman full of promise and possibility and you decided to snuff her out before she could fulfill any of that potential because you wanted to what? Dip your wick at work?"

"Enough." Danielle separated the two men. "Dr. Dolan, I'd like you to come down to headquarters to answer a few questions."

Dolan rounded on her. "Make me, sugar tits." He poked her in the chest with an extended index finger now, too.

Big mistake.

"If you insist," Danielle said. Then she did something to Dolan's index finger and the man was on his knees in front of her begging for mercy. "Ward Dolan, you are under arrest for assaulting an FBI agent. You have the right to remain silent . . ."

CHAPTER TWENTY ONE

Every time Morgan looked at Ward Dolan's face, he wanted to punch it.

He'd had to satisfy himself with occasional glances at Dolan in the back of Danielle's car, hands cuffed and uncomfortable. It would do for now.

Danielle put in her hands-free device and tapped a button on her cell phone. "Hi, Murphy. It's Hernandez. I'm going to need some assistance when I arrive. I'm sending my location now."

She listened for a moment and said, "One suspect being brought in for questioning. See you in a few."

She'd pulled the sedan into the parking garage when they arrived and two agents were waiting for them. Danielle stepped out and tossed the keys to one of them. "Thanks, guys. Interview room 2, okay?"

The men nodded and pulled open the door to the backseat to help Dolan out. Morgan followed Danielle into the building. "I want to stop by our war room to pick up some files."

"Great," Morgan said. "It has to be him. Did you hear how he talked about Lexa and Brianna? Plus, he's a liar. He said he didn't know who they were."

Danielle gave him some side-eye as she strode along the corridor. "Being a creep and a liar doesn't mean he's a murderer." She snorted. "If every creep was a murderer, our population would drop by half. Maybe more here in D.C."

Morgan wasn't ready to joke around about Dolan or sexual predators. Nervous tension shot through him, keeping his hands balled into fists at his side. "So what's our next move here?"

They rounded the corner into the conference room and Danielle gathered up some of the files that were scattered across the desk. "Our next move? Based on how the two of you got along at his house, I think I should take this interview on my own."

Morgan looked down at his feet. He'd let Dolan get to him. That was on him. "I can keep it together. I think I should be there, though. If any of what he says has to do with hospital procedure or medical practices, you won't know if he's lying. I will."

Danielle gazed at him, teeth gnawing at her lower lip. That was her tell. She was thinking about what he'd said. There was a reason she'd brought him into this investigation in the first place. That reason hadn't changed. He knew the hospital. He knew the culture and he was damned good at finding that one little piece of the puzzle that didn't seem to belong, but was the key to making everything come together. He stayed quiet, letting her come to a decision on her own. He held his breath. He wanted to be there when Dolan confessed. Morgan wanted to look the man in his eyes as Dolan owned up to his crimes.

Finally, she took a deep breath and said, "Okay, but you have to keep quiet. Even if he lies about something. You can write me a note so I know how to direct my questions, but I want you to keep your lips zipped for the duration. Do you understand?"

"One hundred percent." He let out the breath he'd been holding.

"Fine. Come with me." Danielle picked up the folders and marched out of the room and down the hall to where the interview rooms were.

One of the agents that had met them in the garage now stood outside the door of the room where Dolan was being held. "He's been pretty quiet."

"Thanks for keeping an eye on him, Mick." Danielle unlocked the door and walked in.

Morgan followed, giving the agent a nod.

It looked like Dolan had fallen asleep. He'd pillowed his arms as best he could with the handcuffs still on and rested his head on them. Morgan had read something somewhere that it's usually the guilty that become very calm when they're arrested. It's a relief to them, in some ways, to be caught. People who are innocent tend to be the ones up, pacing around, demanding lawyers. If that was the case here, Dolan was as guilty as sin.

Dolan looked up as the door shut behind them with a click. "Could I have a glass of water or something?" His eyes were red-rimmed and there was a slight tremble in his hands. Guilt or DTs? Morgan wasn't sure.

"Sure," Danielle said, settling herself in the chair across from Dolan and nodding for Morgan to take a seat next to her. A few seconds later, there was a discreet knock at the door and the agent who had been standing outside before came in with a paper cup of water that he set in front of Dolan, then left without saying word.

If there was any doubt that they were being watched and listened to, that was gone. Morgan wasn't sure if that was a ploy or not.

Danielle set a pad of paper in front of herself and a pen. "So, Dr. Dolan, can you tell us where you've been for the past three days?"

"Every minute of them?"

"If possible."

Dolan took a sip of the water. A little of it sloshed onto the table. "It's possible. Not terribly interesting, but possible."

"I'm listening," Danielle said, pen poised to start writing.

"For the last three days, I've been inside my house. Drinking."

She looked up, eyes narrowed. "Is that supposed to be funny?" The tremble in his hands had gotten worse. He was shaking the water out of the cup.

"No," he said, looking down at them. "Not funny."

Danielle glanced in Morgan's direction. He shrugged. She looked back at Dolan. "I don't think we're following."

Dolan sneered. "Too bad. That's all I've got. I don't remember much of it myself."

He was way too nonchalant. He was hiding something.

Danielle opened the folders and pulled a photo out of each one and then set them up so that Dolan could see them. They were all crime scene photos. Michelle, Brianna, and Lexa. Morgan had to look away. He'd seen plenty of dead bodies in his day. None had touched him like these three.

"And?" Dolan asked. "What do these have to do with me?"

Morgan gritted his teeth. How could Dolan look at those photos and act so nonchalant? These were people, for heaven's sake. Did the man have ice water in his veins?

"It's what we're trying to figure out, Dr. Dolan. Did you know any of these women?" If Danielle's gaze could have cut glass, it would have.

He glanced at the photos and shrugged. "I'd worked a little with Windham and I'd seen Olson around the hospital. The third one I don't recognize at all."

That was all he had to say? No concern for these young women or horror over what had happened to them? Morgan's hands balled into fists under the table.

"Look," Dolan finally said, breaking the silence that Danielle had let drag on. "I've seen the news. I know you've got three women dead who all worked at Georgetown at some point. It hasn't got anything to do with me. Janet left three days ago and I crawled inside a bottle of Scotch and only came out this morning."

Based on the way his hands were shaking, he hadn't crawled too far out of it. Maybe it wasn't ice water in his veins. Maybe it was liquor.

Dolan sat back in his chair. "I can't help you."

Morgan wasn't buying any of it. Dolan was lying. "You're telling us that you've been blind drunk for three days, but you recognize two of these women?"

"That's exactly what I'm saying, Stark." Dolan smirked.

That was it. He'd had it. "Be a man, Dolan. Own your actions. You harassed all three of these women and then when it cost you your job and your marriage, you got revenge on them. You used their instincts to help the injured to lure them into a vulnerable position and then you murdered them." He was on his feet now, leaning over the table and yelling into Dolan's face.

Now Danielle was on her feet, too. "Morgan, be quiet."

He couldn't stop, though. "Lexa was worth ten of you. More. Probably each one of these women was."

Danielle gave him a hard shove toward the door. "Out."

He turned to stare at her. Her face was alight with anger and frustration. "I said out."

Dolan's smirk got bigger. Morgan wanted to wipe it off his face, but realized he wasn't going to win this one, or at least not right then. He held his hands up in front of himself. "I'm going." He stomped to the door. "But I'm not finished with you, Dolan. Not by a long shot."

"Out!" Danielle said. "Now!"

The agent Danielle had called Mick opened the door for Morgan and Danielle flung it shut behind him. The agent gave him a nod and then took up his post in front of the door again.

Morgan paced. What was going on in there? What lies was Dolan spinning? He didn't have to wait long. Danielle emerged from the room only a few minutes later. "Get him a phone, please," she said to the agent. "He wants a lawyer."

The agent nodded and went into the room.

Danielle looked at Morgan, shaking her head. "You. This way."

She strode into the conference room and shut the door behind them.

Morgan sat down at the table and folded his hands in front of himself, trying to contain his anger and frustration. "Look. I'm sorry. It was just so clear he was lying –"

"Was it, Morgan? Was it obvious? Do you know what's going to make it difficult to tell if someone's lying about this case? Giving out information that the general public doesn't have."

Morgan couldn't process what she was saying. "What are you talking about?"

"You told Dolan about our theory that the murderer is luring the woman to him by pretending to be injured. That was a little detail that we could have used to help sort out the crazies from the real deals. Now you've tainted that." She flung herself down in one of the chairs.

Heat crept up his neck. He hadn't considered that.

"Not to mention that, now that you've put him on his back foot, he's not cooperating. He's lawyered up. That was supposed to be an interview. Not an interrogation. Those are two very different things." She stacked the file folders up on the table in front of herself.

"I'm sorry," he said, shame creeping up on him. It wasn't a sensation he was familiar with and he didn't like it. "I didn't know."

Danielle pinched the bridge of her nose as if a headache was coming on. "I realize that. That's why you were supposed to be quiet in there. Remember when we made that agreement, Morgan?"

He did. "I'll do better," he said.

"See that you do," she snapped. "Otherwise, you are off this investigation entirely. I really thought you could help, but not if you're going to behave like this. You could jeopardize the entire case."

"I'll rein it in," he said.

She shook her head. "Go home, Morgan. Cool off. I'll be in touch."

She turned on her heel and marched away, leaving him alone in the hallway, staring after her.

Morgan did as she suggested, making his way home on the Metro. He walked into his apartment, his nostrils assailed by the smell of old food and unwashed plates. It reminded him way too much of the way Dolan's house had looked and smelled.

Screw that. He wasn't Dolan. Washed up sorry excuse for a man.

Well, then, maybe he should stop living like him.

He picked up the empty pizza boxes and take-out containers that were stacked on the kitchen counter and dragged them down to the Dumpster. For a moment, the memory of finding Lexa's lifeless body by the Dumpster in her back alley assailed him. Grief washing over him, making him weak in the knees.

What would Lexa think of how he was behaving now? Was would Fiona think? Moping around. Feeling sorry for himself. Losing control of his emotions. This wasn't the man they'd thought he was. This wasn't the man he wanted to be.

He walked to the nearest grocery story and picked up food. Actual food. Vegetables and fruit. Crusty whole grain bread. Chicken breasts and salmon. Then he came home and cooked. And when he was finished eating, he did the damn dishes.

He looked longingly at the bottle of Scotch and his recliner and then turned his back on them. Nope. That wasn't the way he wanted to live.

The directory of providers that Ashley had given him sat on his dining table. He'd stopped when he hit Dolan. There were twenty-two more letters in the alphabet to get through.

He cracked his knuckles and sat down with the pages.

CHAPTER TWENTY TWO

The man watched the house from the safety of his car across the street. It was a nice neighborhood. Who didn't like Alexandria? Good schools. Property held its value.

Up and down the street, lights came on in kitchens and dining rooms and family rooms as the sun began to set. The day had been warm, truly spring-like. The evening would cool off a bit, but not by much. Still, windows and doors that had been open were being closed. He'd hoped he could slip in unannounced, but that seemed less likely by the moment.

Besides, no lights were coming on in the house he was watching. Where the hell was the doctor?

The MD that was so full of himself, so convinced doctors knew everything, so sure doctors were God.

Idiot.

The man gnawed on the side of his thumb. This wasn't good. He was so close. So close! He'd have worked his way through his list after this one last person. Then his work would be complete. He could relax.

Where. Was. The. Doctor?

The man shot to attention. A car came down the street, signaling a turn into the driveway of the house he was watching. Was it him?

He collapsed back in his seat. No. It was a woman. A blonde. Must be the man's wife.

She pulled into the garage, cut the engine, then the garage door came down. Lights came on inside. With the darkness outside, it was like she was performing a play for him. Acting out putting away groceries, leafing through the mail.

He wished he could change the channel.

So where was his final victim? Not at home. Not at the hospital. He'd already checked there.

He'd have to be patient. He'd find the doctor soon enough. There was not going to be any escape. Not for long.

CHAPTER TWENTY THREE

Morgan had not found any other likely suspects in the directory. Dolan had been the only one who'd left under suspicious circumstances. It had been a long night and his eyes had been burning by the time he went to bed.

He woke the next morning feeling more clear-headed than he had in months. He forced himself out the door to run, something that he'd done four to five days a week when he'd still been with Ashley, but hadn't bothered with for months. His excuses had run the gamut from it being too cold and dark to acknowledging that he was hungover. Not today, though. Today he made his legs turn over and his heart rate rise. He could feel the toxins leaving his system. Not just the booze and the crappy fast food. Some of the anger and hate and grief were going as well. It was all poison.

By the time he hit the door of his apartment building, sweat streamed down the sides of his face and he gasped for air. He'd only run a mile, but it was more than he'd done in quite some time. It would take time to work back up to his usual five-mile runs, but he'd get there.

There would be a new normal. He wasn't sure what it was going to look like yet, but it would come. It wouldn't include Lexa. He doubted it would include Ashley. It would include him, though. He wasn't going anywhere. Sabotaging himself wasn't going to help anyone.

His phone rang as he let himself into the apartment and he looked at the Caller ID. Danielle. Maybe she'd found something on Dolan. Maybe she'd figured out how to nail him. Maybe she'd forgiven him for his poor behavior. "Yes?"

"Hi, Morgan. It looks like Dolan wasn't involved with any of our victims."

Morgan hit the door frame with his fist. "You're sure?" Damn it all to hell. He'd actually wanted it to be that prick.

"I am. I checked the police reports on the harassment claims. There were three young women who accused of Dolan of misconduct, but none of them were our victims. There is no reason that Dolan would go after any our three." She paused. "His alibi, such as it was, checked out, too. Apparently being blind drunk doesn't stop you from ordering take-out food and liquor deliveries. I have several delivery people who dealt with him during crucial time periods and they all remember him. Not fondly, by the way, but still they remember him. Plus his phone never left his home."

"So what do we do now?" Morgan sank down on one of the stools at his breakfast bar and cradled his head in his hands.

"I look for another connection."

"Just you?" Morgan asked, not missing the pronoun she used.

"For now. Why don't you take a day off?"

A day off. What was he supposed to do with a day off? He started to argue, but thought better of it.

They hung up and Morgan headed to the shower. A day off probably wasn't a bad idea. Looking back at his behavior the day before hadn't made him feel very good about himself. He was so used to being an expert on everything around him that he hadn't considered that Danielle would have her reasons for doing things her way.

Perhaps it would be good to get some perspective.

So his hunch about the murderer being a colleague hadn't paid off. There had to be something else, something that he wasn't seeing.

He stripped off his sweaty running clothes and tossed them in the hamper. He switched on the shower and stepped in, letting the hot water run over his head and shoulders.

Brianna was the piece that was throwing him off. When he'd been searching for the link between Lexa and Michelle, Brianna's name had never come up. She hadn't worked with Lexa on any of her cases.

Yet, she'd looked familiar to Morgan. He might not have been able to cough up her name or what case they'd worked on together, but he knew they had.

It hit him as he toweled off. He had worked with Brianna. He had worked with Lexa. He had worked with Michelle. Maybe he was the link between them. Lexa had been working with him for a few months. It was standard operating procedure for attendings to pass off patients to their residents to finish up final paperwork and tests and discharge orders. What if they were still looking for a disgruntled patient or a family member of a patient, but it had really been his patient? Lexa might have only been a name on a piece of paper that the murderer had seen.

Maybe Morgan should have been the target. Not Lexa.

The tsunami of guilt crashed over him and nearly brought him to his knees. What if it was his mistake that had sent a killer seeking vengeance after Lexa? What if it was his fault that she was dead?

CHAPTER TWENTY FOUR

Morgan settled himself behind his computer. He'd managed to get to his office without running into too many people who might question why he was there and what he was doing or, worse yet, anyone who might mention his presence to Ashley. He was pretty sure he'd pushed her as far as he could. He watched the breeze toss the tree tops around as he waited for his computer to boot up.

He stuffed down a slight twinge of unease. He wasn't breaking any rules here. He would only be looking at his own patients. Yet, guilt still gnawed at him. The possibility that it was his own actions that had begun the chain of events that left three young women dead wasn't one he really wanted to entertain.

Yet, he had to.

If there was even the slightest chance that he could stop the chain of violence, he had to take it. Even if it meant facing one of his worst fears.

Fear of his own failure.

He began with the most recent of his patients. Vincenzo Rohr. As he read through the file, all he could see was Lexa's quiet compassion when speaking with Vincenzo's wife about their little girl, the way she was willing to throw herself bodily in front of the charge nurse to let Morgan stop Ayres from starting the operation to clip Vincenzo's aneurysm, her desire to push herself farther so she wouldn't miss a diagnosis the next time.

Nothing in the file pointed to anything that would make someone strike out at Lexa.

He worked backwards. A woman in her 70s was brought in by her daughter. The ER docs thought it was a stroke but couldn't find anything on the CT Scan. Their next thought had been the onset of dementia, but the daughter insisted that her mother had been functioning fine the previous week. Morgan had been called in and while he was fairly certain of the diagnosis, he passed the case on to Lexa to see if she could catch it. It took Lexa only a quick scan of the chart to request a urine test and diagnose the woman with a UTI. After a day on IV fluids to deal with dehydration and antibiotics to deal with the infection, the woman was again oriented in space and time and was ready to be discharged to her own home.

Lexa had caught the problem and diagnosed it quickly, treating the patient in a way that was non-invasive and incredibly effective. No reason to target her for anything there. She'd sat next to the older woman, holding her hand while taking her pulse, talking to her quietly and calmly. The daughter had hugged Lexa when they'd left.

Nothing there. If anything, that family would be looking to put Lexa up for sainthood.

Then he hit pay dirt.

Don Fugate. He'd forgotten about this guy completely, mainly because there wasn't a diagnosis to be made. Morgan had pegged him as a drug seeker within about two minutes. The request for OxyContin by name, the aggressive behavior when questioned about the pain from his supposed back injury, the fact that this was Fugate's third trip to the ER requesting OxyContin in eight weeks. It also hadn't escaped Morgan that while Fugate got confrontational and belligerent with him, he'd been polite and appropriate with the female nurse who had taken his vitals. He checked to see who that was and pushed back from the computer for a second when he saw that the nurse was Brianna Olson. There was the connection.

Morgan had passed Fugate onto Lexa, assuming Fugate would keep up his more docile ways and wanting Lexa to get some experience with drug-seekers. She'd have to deal with them eventually. They were a reality of any Emergency Department in the country.

That sharp pang hit him again. Lexa wouldn't have to deal with anything, now. If Fugate was the one who killed Lexa because Morgan had passed a difficult patient onto his resident as a learning experience, he wasn't sure what he'd do.

Morgan flipped through the chart. Michelle's name wasn't in the chart, but that meant nothing. She still could have been the tech to process Fugate's lab work. The techs didn't always put their names on test results. Fugate had seen both Brianna and Lexa. Maybe Michelle had come up to collect samples. That wasn't out of the question. He could have seen all three young women and then followed them when they left the hospital. He wouldn't even have to know their names.

Morgan closed the file and pushed his chair back from the desk, leaning back to stare at the ceiling while he thought. Lexa had talked about this patient afterwards. She'd been surprised at the man's vehemence about needing a specific drug and how angry he'd become when she wouldn't prescribe it. She'd wanted Morgan's advice on how she might have better dealt with him. It had saddened him then that there really wasn't an answer to that question. There wasn't a good choice.

In the end, Security had to remove Fugate from the ER, ranting and raving paranoid fantasies about the entire medical establishment being against him and no one caring about whether or not he was in pain because he was an ex-con.

Morgan sat bolt upright. An ex-con. Could the man have been violent before? If there was a history of violence coupled with drug addiction, who knows what could happen? It was a recipe for heartache, that was for sure.

He pulled out his phone and called Danielle. She answered on the third ring, sounding weary. "What is it, Morgan?"

He ignored her lack of enthusiasm. "I have someone I think we should check out, someone with connections to Brianna and Lexa and maybe to Michelle."

There was a pause. "I'm listening." She sounded much more enthusiastic.

"A patient I passed off to Lexa because I thought it would be a good learning experience." He had to stop for a second to get control of his emotions. "He was angling for an OxyContin prescription that he clearly didn't need. Lexa mentioned later that he'd gotten pretty worked up when she wouldn't write him a prescription. He had to be removed by Security."

"Okay," Danielle said.

"I think someone mentioned the guy was an ex-con," he said.

There was silence for a moment on Danielle's end. Was she blowing him off? Did she not want his help anymore?

"Spell the name for me again," she said.

He did and then heard the sound of computer keys clicking, then a slight hiss of breath being released.

That had to mean something. "What?" he asked.

"Mr. Fugate did hard time for assault with a deadly weapon. He was lucky."

"How is that lucky?" Didn't sound that way to Morgan.

"They could easily have charged him with attempted homicide based on what I'm reading here. He must have made a deal." There was another pause. "Hold on for a minute, Morgan?"

“Sure.” Morgan swiveled around in his office chair as he waited for Danielle. It was a typical doctor’s office. His framed diplomas hung on one wall. A photo of Ashley sat on the credenza behind him so she was the first thing he saw when he walked in. The other wall had a painting of a seascape, impressionistic enough that it was almost abstract, but with an illusion of depth that patients seemed to find comforting. He’d often see people gazing into it as he gave them difficult diagnoses. Ashley had picked it out, of course.

“Morgan?” Danielle was back. “I just spoke to Fugate’s parole officer. He has a job on a construction site in Falls Church. He should be there now. I’ll pick you up in twenty minutes.”

CHAPTER TWENTY FIVE

Morgan got out of the sedan that Danielle had parked behind a line of cars along a chain link fence that had to be at least ten feet high with a coil of razor wire over that. She got out as well, checking her pockets and her holster. “Let’s set some ground rules.”

“I’m listening.” Morgan stuffed his hands into his pockets.

“I want you here because of your eye for detail, your powers of observation, the way you have of picking out some telling element of what’s in front of you that most people miss.”

He understood that. It’s why he got called in by so many other doctors to consult on tricky cases. It was something innate, something he hadn’t realized was special until he’d started his residency. One of the first attendings he’d worked with – a man named Monte Flint – had been the one to point it out to him. He’d helped steer Morgan’s career in the direction it had gone, convinced that Morgan had something unique to offer his patients.

He hadn’t been wrong.

“I’ll keep my eyes, ears, and nose peeled,” Morgan told Danielle.

“Good. That’s what I need. What I don’t need is for you to tackle the person we’re here to talk to. I don’t need you to threaten him or to accuse him of anything.” She put her sunglasses on. “Got it?”

Morgan nodded. “Got it.”

“Good. Now let’s go find out where this Fugate guy is.” She marched to where part of the fence had been rolled back to make a gate and then up the steps of a trailer that had a small red ‘office’ sign on it.

She pounded on it three times in short succession and then stepped back. Nothing happened so she pounded again. This time the door flew open. “What the . . .?” The man in front of them let his words trail off at the sight of Danielle. He was a light-skinned Black man with greenish eyes and a very close-cropped goatee. He looked wiry and wore a button-down tucked into belted jeans.

Danielle held up her badge. “I’d like to ask one of your employees some questions.”

The man’s eyes narrowed. “Is this about the copper wire?”

Danielle shook her head. "You been having a problem with your copper wire?"

The man sighed and motioned for them to come into the small cramped office space. "Only if I actually want to get this job finished on time and on budget." He sat. "Which I do," he added. "So who do you want to talk to? I'll page whoever it is." He lifted the handset of the phone on his desk.

Danielle held up her hand. "I'd rather if we approached him in person than paging him, if that's okay, Mr. —."

"Hawes. Nathaniel Hawes. And you are?"

"Agent Danielle Hernandez and this is Morgan Stark. He's consulting with us on this case." She sat back in her chair, waiting.

Hawes sat back as well and regarded them both. "This is an active construction site. It's not safe for people to be traipsing around here. It's easy to get hurt."

"I assure you, we will not be traipsing anywhere," Danielle said, a hint of a smile playing on her lips. "We're happy to be escorted to the area where our subject is. I'd just prefer not to give him advance warning."

Hawes nodded. "Sure. We can probably do that. Who are you looking for?"

"Don Fugate."

Hawes looked slightly surprised. "Don? Really? What's he done?"

"I don't know that he's done anything, Mr. Hawes. I'd just like to speak to him." Danielle glanced sideways at Morgan as if to warn him to keep his mouth shut. Morgan got the hint and stayed silent.

Hawes regarded them for a moment and then nodded. He stood and grabbed two hardhats and two orange safety vests from the shelves behind him and shoved them across the desk at Danielle and Morgan. "You'll have to wear these."

"Happy to," Danielle said, jamming the bright yellow hardhat onto her head. Morgan followed suit, feeling a little as if he was playing dress up, first as an FBI consultant and now as a construction worker.

Hawes led them out of the trailer and down into the construction site. Danielle kept pace with him while Morgan trailed a step or two behind, taking in all the commotion. The noise was constant. Machinery and the banging of hammers. Everything smelled like diesel fuel and dust. To Morgan's eyes, the place looked like a jumble of people and machinery and supplies, but Hawes led them through the site, striding confidently and waving occasionally at different people.

He stopped about 15 yards from where two men, both wearing hardhats leaned over a trestle table. "Don's the one on the right."

Morgan might have recognized him, but was happy he didn't have to pick him out of the crowd. A forklift drove between them and the man they were looking for. He glanced their way, but quickly looked back at the plans on the table.

Danielle waited until the forklift was past and then strode up and tapped the man on the shoulder while Morgan hung back, not wanting Fugate to see him and recognize him yet. Fugate turned, a confused look on his face. Confusion turned to fear the second Danielle held up her badge. Fugate shoved the other man aside and ran.

"Damn it." Danielle took off after Fugate, yelling "Stay here, Morgan!" as she went, her ponytail streaming out behind her.

Morgan rushed over to the table, helping the other man to right himself. How the hell was he supposed to just stand here while Danielle ran through a construction site on the trail of a murderer? In front of Morgan on the table was a blueprint of the building site. Morgan looked down at it. Years of looking at X-rays and scans had trained his mind to look at a two-dimensional image and extrapolate to the three-dimensional reality. He might not be an architect or a construction manager, but the schematic before him was, in many ways, no different than looking at an MRI.

Ahead, he saw Fugate running into the half-finished building with Danielle right behind him.

In Morgan's head, the whole building rose before him almost as if it was a movie.

There were limited places for Fugate to go once he made that turn into the building. He'd trapped himself like a rat in a maze. Either Danielle would corner him or he'd emerge from the lower level entrance on the east side of the building.

Morgan jabbed his finger at that back entrance on the blueprint and turned to the foreman. "Is there a way through the outer fencing from here? Or would he have to come back this way to get off the property?"

The foreman looked at him blankly. "What?"

Morgan gritted his teeth and just barely kept himself from grabbing the man from the shoulders and shaking him. "The outer fencing. Is there another way out besides the main entrance?"

"Yeah, but you'd have to have a key." The blank look remained.

"Does Fugate have one?"

"Sure. All the employees—"

Morgan didn't wait to hear the rest of the man's words. If Fugate had a key, he could duck out one of the back entrances and Danielle might lose him. Morgan took off running, heading toward the southwest corner of the building. Looking up, he thought he saw a flash of orange moving fast. He'd been right about the direction Fugate would have to go.

The cacophony of the building site made it nearly impossible for him to keep track of where Danielle and Fugate were by noise, but then he heard someone shout to look out. It had to be them. Morgan kept going.

He ducked beneath a girder hanging from a crane and rounded the first corner, nearly running into a pile of cement blocks. He skidded around them, scraping up against them as he went. Someone shouted for him to watch it, but there was no time to check behind him. There were fewer obstacles on this side of the building, but he'd lost precious moments scanning the blueprint. He increased his pace, leaping over a stack of wooden slats.

"Stop! FBI!" Danielle's yell echoed out of the concrete and steel structure. Fugate was headed this way. Morgan was sure. His instincts had been right.

He rounded the next corner and twisted his way through piles of steel girders, stacks of drywall, and sacks of concrete. There was an open area ahead of him. It had to be the back entrance. Twisting around a forklift, he ran straight at it.

And found Don Fugate running straight at him. Morgan stopped dead in Fugate's path.

A look of confusion crossed the man's face for a second, but only for a second. Then he shifted to go around Morgan.

That second of hesitation was all Danielle needed, though. She grabbed his arm and in a quick fluid motion had Fugate down on his knees in the dust. Chest heaving, she said, "Don Fugate, you are under arrest for violating parole. "

Morgan bent over, hands on thighs, to catch his breath.

"You okay?" Danielle asked as she snapped the cuffs on Fugate.

"Fine," he panted, noticing that she was already catching her breath while he was still laboring.

"You sure about that? You're bleeding."

***

It turned out the blood had come from scraping up against the concrete blocks. It was nothing more than an abrasion, but Danielle's tight-lipped look at him as a young EMT at the local precinct cleaned and bandaged it told Morgan that he wasn't going to get to blow it off and deal with it himself later.

They were in one of the interrogation rooms. It wasn't as nice as the one at FBI Headquarters. Not that that one was the Ritz or anything. This one had a bit of a smell to it, though. Some unholy combination of sweat and fear with an underpinning of urine.

Morgan checked over the job the young woman with the braided pigtails had done on his arm. Not half bad. He flexed his arm and rotated his shoulder. It'd do. "Thanks," he told her.

She gave him a nod. "You're going to want to put some antibiotic cream on it. Just in case."

"Got it," he assured her, barely managing to keep himself from rolling his eyes.

As soon as the door clicked shut behind the young woman, Danielle sat down on the table next to where he sat. "What the hell were you thinking this time, Morgan? He had on heavy boots. There wasn't an unfair advantage this time."

What had he been thinking? "I wanted to slow him down a bit." And he'd known he could do it. He could see exactly what was going to happen and how he could help. It had worked, too.

She sighed and stood. "Well, you did that. You realize you've created a stack of paperwork for me now, though." She pointed at the bandage on his arm.

He winced. He knew exactly what that was like. "Sorry."

"It's okay." She paced the small room. "I think you should sit out this interview, though."

"No way!" Morgan protested. "Why?"

She shot him some side-eye. "It's not your call to make, Morgan. It's mine. And you haven't stayed particularly calm through our other interviews."

"Give me the ground rules. I'll stick to them." He'd try, at least.

"Like you did at the construction site?"

"Hey! I didn't tackle him. I didn't accuse him of anything or call him a liar."

Danielle snorted. "So you didn't. Okay, but you have got to keep it together or I can't have you in here. Understand?"

"One hundred percent."

The door opened and a uniformed officer brought in a handcuffed Fugate. "He's been processed. He's yours for now. Let me know if you need anything else, Agent Hernandez."

"Will do. Thanks, Tony."

The officer pulled a chair out for Fugate and helped him sit. Danielle came around the table and sat down next to Morgan. "So, Mr. Fugate, can you tell me where you were on the nights of April 22nd, April 24th, and April 25th?"

Fugate frowned. He had a thick brow that creased, nearly overshadowing his eyes. "When? Why?"

"Please just answer the questions."

"I don't know where I was those first two days, but on Thursday night I was at Petey's with some guys from the job site. It's play-offs." He said it as if everyone should have known that.

Right. Basketball. Petey's must be a sports bar.

"Anyone who can verify that?" Danielle asked, her pen poised over her notebook.

"Sure. Nate Sepulveda, Harlan Loy, Vito Olmstead, Robbie Seeley." He lifted up a finger for each name he listed.

Danielle jotted them down and then shut her book. She tapped a few items into her phone as well.

"That's it?" Fugate asked, jaw dropped a bit. The man was a total mouth breather. "You chased me down and hauled me in here to check on my social calendar?"

Danielle stayed very still. "Not exactly. Tell us about your relationship with Lexa Windham."

"My what with who?" Fugate's eyes bugged a little.

"Your relationship with Lexa Windham." Danielle spoke each work slowly, carefully enunciating.

Fugate frowned. "I ain't dim. You don't have to talk to me like that."

"Great. Any chance you could answer the question?" Danielle leaned back, taking a more relaxed pose.

"I don't even know who that is. No way I have any kind of thing going with a chick named Lexa." Fugate shook his head.

Morgan felt the steam rising in his head. He leaned forward, getting his face right into Fugate's. "She wasn't some chick. She was a person. A young woman who already had accomplished more than what you'll probably do in your whole sorry excuse for a life."

Danielle tugged him back and gave him a warning look. "Dr. Windham treated you at Georgetown University Hospital in March."

Realization dawned on Fugate's face. He turned to Morgan. "I knew you looked familiar! You passed me off to the chick doctor who wouldn't do anything for my back."

"Because you don't have a back problem, Fugate," Morgan shot back. "You have an Oxy problem."

Fugate ignored Morgan and turned to Danielle. "So what's the deal with this Lexa chick. Why do you want to know about her?"

"Do you watch the news, Mr. Fugate?" Danielle asked.

He shook his head. "Not if I can help it."

"Lexa Windham was murdered on April 24th. The nurse who helped her treat you – Brianna Olson – was murdered on April 25th." Danielle said the words calmly, but they made Morgan's blood boil. All that potential, gone, because of an idiot like Fugate.

All the blood drained from Fugate's face. "And you think I had something to do with that? No. No. No. No. Absolutely not."

Danielle steepled her hand in front of herself. "You were pretty angry when you left the Emergency Department that night. According to witnesses, you threatened Dr. Windham and pretty much everyone else you saw."

"I was just blowing off steam. I was in pain and nobody would help. You don't know what it's like to have a back that hurts like that." Fugate's voice was developing a whine.

"Yet you seem to be able to do your job at the construction site pretty well and you certainly can run." Danielle leaned in. "And why was that, Mr. Fugate? Why did you run?"

Fugate dropped his head into his hands. "I don't believe this. I can't freaking win."

"What can't you win, Mr. Fugate?" Danielle's voice had gotten even quieter and softer.

"I'm damned if I do and damned if I don't."

To Morgan's disgust, the man's eyes filled with tears. The man was throwing himself a pity party while Lexa lay dead in the morgue. Morgan shoved back from the table and crossed his arms over his chest, but he kept his mouth shut.

"How are you damned?" Danielle asked.

Morgan didn't know how she did it, how she kept her cool like that.

"I . . . I thought you were there because . . ." He brushed a tear off his cheek with the back of his forearm.

“Because why, Don?”

It didn’t escape Morgan that she’d switched to the man’s first name.

“I did some blow the other night, the night I was out with the guys watching the game. I ran into some dude in the bathroom and he offered me a line and I did it. I thought you were there to drug test me and I panicked.” His face fully crumpled now. “I don’t want to go back inside.”

Ridiculous. The man was clearly lying.

“You do realize that running from the FBI is a really good way to make sure you’ll get drug tested, right?” Danielle pointed out.

“I said I panicked! I wasn’t thinking! I just wanted to get away.”

Danielle’s phone beeped and she squinted at it for a moment and then sighed. “Okay, Mr. Fugate. Your alibi checks out. The bartender at Pete’s remembers you being there that night. Not for any flattering reasons, though. You’re not a very nice customer, apparently. You’re not welcome back there. ”

“So what does that mean?” Fugate asked.

Danielle reached across the table and unlocked the handcuffs. “It means you’re free to go.”

“Wait! What?” Morgan swiveled in his chair to stare at her. “He’s an addict. Addicts lie all the time. He’s making all this up. He’s got specific connections to two of the victims. Probably to the first one, too. I just haven’t found it yet.”

“He’s also got an alibi, Morgan. He’s not our guy.” Danielle held up a hand to stop him.

“He is!” Not another one. Not another one where they got so close and then had to let him get away. Morgan pounded his fists on the table and then pointed at Fugate who shrunk away from him. “Did you kill her because she wouldn’t give you drugs? Because she knew you were trying to play the system? Did you figure out where she lived? Maybe followed her after she’d spent a long day saving lives at the hospital? Is that what you did?”

Fugate shook his head. “No, man. I swear. I didn’t touch that chick.”

“STOP CALLING HER THAT!! Her name was Lexa Windham.” Morgan felt the tears clog in his throat and then Danielle was in his face.

“Out,” she whispered at him. “Now.”

Chastened, he got up and walked out of the room, but not without a backwards glare at Fugate. “What?” he said as they got outside.

"Go home, Morgan. You're overwrought."

He leaned back against the wall and consciously relaxed his shoulders. She had a point. He hadn't kept his cool. "Fine. I'll go. What time should I meet you tomorrow?"

"You shouldn't. I . . . I was wrong. You don't belong in an investigation like this. You were too close to Lexa. I can't have you jeopardizing my case like this." She looked down at the floor and then back up at him. "I'm sorry."

He couldn't believe what he was hearing. "Jeopardizing? I helped you catch both Fugate and Dolan, remember?" Not to mention finding the names in the first place.

"At what cost, Morgan? I need you off this case before you hurt yourself or someone else. You're breaking rules left and right. What good will it be to catch the person actually responsible if I can't put them away?" She shook her head. "We're done. You're done. It's been nice knowing you." She turned on her heel and went back into the interrogation room.

Morgan stood in the hallway, staring after her.

Danielle might be done with him, but he was far from done with this case.

CHAPTER TWENTY SIX

Morgan got on the Metro to go home. It wasn't rush hour yet, but the trains were still crowded with people. He grabbed a strap and braced himself for the jolting ride.

People were all around him. Women in business suits carrying attaché cases, men in khakis and button-downs, young moms with little kids to corral. Noise and movement surrounded him, yet he felt curiously separate from it all.

None of it touched him. None of it connected with him. He'd never felt this alone. Not after Fiona died. Not after his parents died, one after the other. Not even when Ashley asked him to move out. He hadn't fully realized how much he'd been leaning on this investigation to get him through the day. Without it, everything rushed in. All the doubts and fears and fatigue swamped him.

Medicine had always been there for him to turn to, immersing himself in figuring out tricky diagnoses or finding new ways to treat patients. That had kept him connected to humanity, his own and the rest of the world's.

Now he felt untethered.

There'd been a rush when he'd thought he'd found the person who killed Lexa and Michelle and Brianna. Each time he thought he'd come up with the answer, he'd gotten that surge, some heady combination of adrenaline and endorphins and serotonin and oxytocin.

He'd been mistaken, though. Morgan hated to face that. He'd really thought he'd found the answer with Fugate. Just as he had with Dolan and Connor. It had been like making a diagnosis. He could see all the different pieces and they'd fallen into place to make a definable picture.

Except the picture had been wrong.

He should be relieved that he was wrong about Fugate. If he'd been right, it would have meant that he'd set in motion the series of events that had led to all those deaths. How would he have been able to live with himself? He could barely stand to live with himself now.

While he had a better than decent track record with his diagnoses, there were times when his first hypotheses proved to not be correct. He'd run a test and end up with a different outcome than he expected.

Oftentimes it gave him more information that led him to the correct answer, a trail of breadcrumbs that led him away from the witch and out of the forest.

Why was this so different?

He felt more defeated now than he ever had when having to start over in making a difficult diagnosis. He got off at his Metro stop and trudged to his apartment building. Standing outside, he couldn't bring himself to go in to brave the stale corridors and his sterile apartment. There was nothing there for him.

There was nothing anywhere for him.

He had no family left. His marriage was over. He'd put his job in jeopardy. Where could he turn?

He cast back through his life for someone, anyone, that he could turn to in a time of trouble. Someone that could guide him through his jumbled thought process. It had been so long since he'd needed that kind of guidance, he could barely remember.

He froze on the sidewalk next to his car. Monte Flint. That was someone he could go to. The man who had put him on the path to the doctor he had become.

Flint had been an attending physician when Morgan had been a lowly resident himself, still trying to figure out what his specialty should be, still trying to figure out what kind of doctor he should be, still trying to figure out what kind of man he should be. Monte Flint had taken Morgan under his wing and had helped him find all those answers.

Even though he'd retired a few years ago, Morgan was fairly certain Monte still lived in the rambling old Tudor in the Woodland-Normanstone Terrace neighborhood where he'd occasionally entertained his residents. At this time of day, the drive would take Morgan easily forty-five minutes. Maybe his head would clear as he went.

He got in his car and plunged into D.C. traffic. Out of habit, he snapped on the radio as he drove. It was tuned to a local news station which, of course, led with the story of three young women having been murdered in similar fashions.

Morgan didn't think Danielle had released any information to the media about her suspicions of a serial killer, but the reporters weren't stupid. It hadn't taken them long to put it all together. There was a note of excitement in the reporter's voice that made Morgan's stomach turn. To the media, this was like catnip to cats. After all, if it bleeds, it leads.

Every time they mentioned Lexa's name, Morgan's chest hurt. Every mention made him remember finding her behind that Dumpster. Every new tidbit of information made him see her on that cold slab in the morgue.

He snapped the radio off. Better to live with the silence.

When he finally pulled onto Monte's street, he drove slowly by the house, a feeling relief swelling in his chest when he saw lights on inside. He found a parking place and stopped for a moment. He got out of the car and leaned against it for a moment. What was he doing here? What did he think could be accomplished? Then he had to face it.

He was here because he didn't feel like he had any other place to go. Was this his version of rock bottom?

He walked up the sidewalk to the front door and rang the bell. A minute later, Monte Flint opened the front door and peered out through the screen. "Morgan?"

Morgan was gratified and relieved that it took his old mentor only a few seconds to recognize and place him. "Hi, Monte. I know I should have called first, but I came by kind of on a whim." Whim wasn't the right word. Crisis? Breakdown? It didn't seem like the right way to kick off the conversation.

Monte opened the door wider and waved him in. Monte still sported a thick head of hair although it was now nearly white, not the salt and pepper that Morgan remembered. He still had a neatly trimmed mustache and just a touch of stubble on his chin. "Don't be ridiculous. I'm happy to see you. Come in. Come in. I just put a pot of coffee on. Would you like a cup?" Monte leaned in and whispered. "It's decaf. Ramon thinks I don't know he swapped it out."

Morgan laughed. Some things never changed. Monte's husband Ramon was a professor of Spanish Literature at American University, but was more in tune with what would keep the two of them healthy than Monte was, despite Monte being a doctor. "I'd love a cup."

Monte led Morgan through the living and dining room to the kitchen. Morgan settled himself on a stool at the marble-topped breakfast bar. Although all the dishes were done, the aromas of the night's dinner hung in the air. It was a homey smell, nothing like the stale air in his apartment.

Ramon poked his head in, dark brown eyes bright behind the reading glasses perched on the tip of his nose and one finger holding his place in a book. His hairline had receded more than Monte's had, but he still looked strong and vital. "Who was at the door?" Then he spotted Morgan at the counter. “Morgan Stark? What a delight! What brings you here to us tonight?”

“He hasn’t said yet, Ramon,” Monte said. “I’m giving him coffee first.”

“Yes, yes. I see. Perhaps a cookie as well?” He opened a cupboard and moved several boxes around before pulling out some shortbread cookies.

“Thanks.” Morgan’s stomach rumbled. A reminder that the day had been so action-packed that he hadn’t really eaten. He’d been that wrapped up in chasing down Don Fugate. And for what?

Ramon laid the cookies out on a plate and set them on the counter. “I’ll let you two catch up.” And with a wave left them on their own.

“He thinks I don’t know where the cookies are either.” Monte set a mug down in front of Morgan and then a pitcher of cream and a sugar bowl on the counter between them.

The tenderness between the two men nearly made Morgan weep. How many little things like this had Ashely done for him? He knew the answer to how many he’d done for her. Pretty close to zero. He poured some cream into his coffee and watched as convection made the two fluids swirl together.

“Now, what’s going on that you’re looking to spend part of your evening with two old men?” Monte took a sip of his coffee and waited.

He’d always been like this. Patient. Calm. Truly listening, not just waiting for his turn to talk. Morgan couldn’t say that about very many attending physicians that he knew. Hell, he wasn’t sure he could say it about himself. He appreciated it in Monte. “I’m not really sure,” he answered.

“Ah. How about filling me in on what’s been happening over the past few days?”

Morgan rolled his shoulders, trying to figure out where to begin. “One of my residents was murdered.”

Monte’s eyebrows shot up. “The young woman who’s been on the news? She was your student?”

“I found her.” Morgan shut his eyes as if that would block out the mental image of Lexa’s bloodied body. “It . . it really threw me for a loop, Monte. I couldn’t seem to concentrate so I decided to take some time off.”

“Smart.” Monte nodded. “We need to be focused when we’re on duty. We owe that to our patients.”

He knew Monte would understand. "Then the FBI agent working the case—"

"FBI?" Monte cut him off. "Why is the FBI involved?"

"There have now been three murders that she thinks are linked." Morgan let that information sink in. "Anyway, she asked me to consult on the case. Since I wasn't doing anything else, well, it seemed like a good idea. Plus I had a different way of looking at things than the FBI did. I've come up with three different suspects, but none of them have panned out. Each time, I get more frustrated and apparently overstep my boundaries. Now she wants me off the case. I don't know how I can step away, though."

Monte scratched the back of his head and made a humming noise for a second. "So this FBI agent asks you to help and out of the goodness of your heart you say yes."

Morgan made a little noise. He wasn't sure the goodness of his heart had anything to do with it, but that really wasn't the point and he knew it.

Monte smiled. "Bear with me. Then the FBI agent says your help is no longer required. It seems like that lets you off the hook."

Morgan shook his head. "I don't want to be off the hook. I want to find this guy and put a stop to whatever is happening here. It's bad enough to have lost Lexa. Who might be next?"

"That's a reasonable question. I'm just not sure it's yours to answer." Monte took a bite of a cookie. "Why do you think it is?"

Why did he feel so responsible? Of course some of it had to do with feeling responsible for Lexa, in general. She'd been his resident, his student to guide. Had he guided her to something that had taken her life? Finding whoever killed her wouldn't bring her back. He knew that. Finding out who and why might bring him some modicum of peace, though.

There was more to it than that, though. He couldn't completely discount the fact that Lexa had reminded him so much of Fiona. He shut his eyes. Another young woman he should have protected, but hadn't. "Because I should have been able to stop it from happening. I should have protected her."

Monte made a show of sniffing Morgan's coffee mug. "What have you been drinking, son? How on earth could you have stopped this?"

Morgan ran his hand over his face, looking for the words that matched the roiling emotions in his gut. "It's like when a tricky case comes across my desk. I didn't set in motion the wheels that caused the person to develop whatever illness or syndrome they have, but I can stop it from getting any worse. I've got the same feeling now that I get when I miss a diagnosis, when I go the wrong direction and don't get a patient the treatment they need in time."

Monte pushed the plate of cookies away from himself and leaned back in his chair, crossing his arms over his chest. "We're human, Morgan. As much as we wish we weren't. As much as some doctors think they're not." He gave a little snort. "We make mistakes."

"And other people pay for them." Morgan turned his coffee cup around in a circle on the table. There were plenty of professions where making a mistake might be unfortunate. In Morgan's world, a mistake might mean someone lost their life or suffered terrible consequences.

His hand froze on his cup. A mistake. A mistake that cost someone dearly. He'd been looking at cases where people had been diagnosed accurately. What about cases where someone hadn't been? And that had somehow led to negative outcomes. He hadn't looked at that yet.

He shoved his chair back and stood. "Monte, as always, you've helped me see this so much more clearly. Thank you."

Monte's eyebrows went up. "I did?"

"Absolutely. I think I know why this person is doing what they're doing and once I know why, I'll be able to figure out who." He picked up his coat and headed toward the front door.

"That wasn't exactly my intention." Monte followed after him.

Morgan turned to face him. "I know. I understand what you're trying to tell me, too. I swear I will take the time to figure out what's driving me after we catch this guy."

"Where are you going now?" Monte asked.

"Back to the hospital."

CHAPTER TWENTY SEVEN

Traffic had cleared by the time Morgan left Monte's house and he made good time getting back to the hospital. He parked in the visitors' section of the parking lot, preferring that as few people as possible know about this little visit.

After all, he'd come here intending to do exactly what he'd told Ashley he wouldn't do. He was going to use his privileges at the hospital to find a misdiagnosis. He gritted his teeth. One more promise to Ashley that he was going to break. None of the other ones had ever been about their professional lives, though. This one would stand alone.

When she found out – if she found out – it would probably be the end of any hope of reconciliation. Not that there was much of that left anyway. Maybe it wouldn't, though. If she understood what he was trying to achieve. She might not approve of his methods, but she'd see why he had to do what he was about to do.

Whatever the misdiagnosis was, it was going to have to be a doozy of a mistake, one so bad that it pushed a person over the edge, pushed them to the point where they would take several other people's lives as revenge. The garage echoed with the sound of a car taking a corner too quickly. The smell of exhaust made his temple twinge.

Morgan flashed his badge at the security guard as he walked into the hospital.

"Late to be coming into work, doc," the man said.

"No rest for the wicked," Morgan replied, trying to sound nonchalant. The last thing he wanted was for anyone to note and remember that he'd been here.

"Ain't that the truth." The man turned back to his phone and Morgan breathed a sigh of relief as he made his way through the halls.

The hospital was always busy. People don't get sick on a timetable, but the administrative offices were generally quiet at night. Separated as they were from the actual wards, lights were dimmed at night in the hallways. Shadows gathered in doorways and his footsteps echoed. Twice he was certain someone was behind him, but no one was there when he whirled around.

Paranoia. It was probably his own sense of guilt making him feel pursued. He knew what he was about to do was wrong. Violating people's privacy had a host of unintended consequences. This time, surely, it would be worth it, though. People would understand once the actual perpetrator was brought to justice. They wouldn't be able to argue with his methods then.

He unlocked the outer door to the exam rooms and offices he shared with three other doctors. He went through the darkened waiting room where patients checked in. The HVAC turned on with a click, ruffling pages of magazines scattered around on tables. Then he went into the small suite of offices and exam rooms. Unlocking the door to his own office, he let himself in, heaving a sigh of relief when he shut the door behind him.

He booted up the computer and entered in his credentials, relieved when the recordkeeping system came up. He'd been a little worried that Ashley would put a flag on him and make it difficult to access the records. He had a feeling that the only reason she hadn't was because of the loyalty she still felt toward him.

It was something.

He flexed his fingers thinking about how to run a search to get what it was he was looking for. He needed someone who'd been misdiagnosed and who had some connection with Michelle, Lexa, and Brianna. The misdiagnosis had to be bad enough for someone to think it was worth murdering three people.

He decided to start with M&M conferences. Anytime there was an adverse outcome for a patient that could have been avoided, the hospital ran a Mortality and Morbidity – commonly referred to as an M&M – conference. A task force made up of doctors from different disciplines would review cases to find if mistakes were made, why they were made, and if there were any way to avoid the same set of mistakes in the future; then they would present their findings. They weren't a matter of finger pointing or trying to assign blame. Their purpose was to elevate the level of care the hospital gave to patients.

Morgan pulled up the agendas for the last three M&Ms and scanned through them quickly. Nothing jumped out at him. Yes. There were mistakes. Yes. Some of them even contributed to the premature death of a patient. Most, however, only accelerated the inevitable. He didn't think any of them were what he was looking for.

He shoved back from his desk and paced his office. Where should he look next? He stopped to gaze out the window. From his vantage point, he could hear the sound of an ambulance arriving at the Emergency Department even if he couldn't see it. He sighed. It meant somebody was having what might well be the worst day of their lives even if it was just another day for the staff.

Realization dawned and Morgan shook his head. He was thinking like a doctor. He'd taken that big step backward that allowed him the objectivity he needed when treating a patient. That was all fine and well while he was working, but that wasn't what was needed now. He needed to think like the killer now. When it's the person you love, what seems like an acceptable error to someone else, might not seem that way to you at all.

He went back through the M&M cases again. Still, nothing rose to the level that would lead someone to take revenge in his opinion. Some family members probably didn't even know that a mistake had been made. Hospitals generally didn't advertise that information.

"Oh, hey, Dr. M!"

Morgan looked up, surprised to see Riley, the person from the cleaning service who always took care of these offices.

"Sorry," she said. "Didn't mean to startle you. I didn't expect anyone to be here right now. Okay if I empty the garbage?"

Morgan darkened the computer screen and then pushed back from his desk. "No problem."

"What are you doing here so late?" Riley asked, wheeling the pushcart in and emptying the smaller trashcan by the desk into it. "You got a tricky one you're working on?"

"I guess you could say that."

"I'll let you get back to it then. G'night."

She trundled out of the room. Morgan waited a few seconds before switching the screen back on and got back to his search. What would lead someone to feel that they needed to take revenge in the form of actual murder? It would have to be bad. Really bad.

Even so, someone wouldn't go directly to murder. They'd try other more common means first, wouldn't they? Lawsuits were the most common way people tried to get satisfaction after some kind of medical mishap. Maybe someone hadn't gotten satisfaction that way and had escalated.

America is a litigious society. People file law suits for all kinds of reasons, some legitimate, some not. Regardless, once a lawsuit was filed, it was public knowledge.

Morgan got back on the computer and began searching for lawsuits filed against Georgetown University Hospital in the past year. There were plenty. About half of them were settled out of court. Not surprising, really. If the hospital knew they'd done something wrong, it was a hell of a lot better to settle things quietly without a lot of fanfare. Patients or their families occasionally signed non-disclosure agreements as part of those settlements so the information would go no further. Other cases, they settled because the expense and hassle of going to court would be greater than the cost of handing over some cash.

Morgan hated those cases. Probably every doctor did. It felt like admitting wrong-doing when there wasn't any.

Of the half that was left, only a very small number went to trial. Most of those cases were dropped or dismissed before they got off the ground. Despite more and more people filing malpractice claims, they were very hard to prove. A lot of times the evidence is extremely technical and complex. It's hard for laypeople to follow the information and unfamiliar lingo. Juries get confused. Put the right expert witness on the stand and it didn't always matter if they were right or wrong. Plus, the plaintiff has to prove actual negligence. It was a high bar to reach.

Morgan looked down the list of suits that had been filed against the hospital that had never gotten off the ground. Most of them were for things that didn't rise to the level of a lawsuit much less revenge killings. A medication mishap that had triggered an allergic reaction, but had been quickly noticed and treated. A miscalculation on a radiation dosage that had caused a burn. Unpleasant, yes, but also quickly treated and resolved.

Then Morgan hit Mary Pickett. That one he'd at least heard about through the hospital grapevine. He hadn't paid much attention at the time. It hadn't been anyone on his service or one of his patients. He remembered the whispers, though. The crazy thing was that it hadn't been a mistake or a misdiagnosis on the part of the medical team. This mix up had happened in the medical billing department.

Mary Pickett had been a white woman in her mid-fifties. She'd come in slightly jaundiced and with abdominal pain. She'd gone through a series of imaging tests at the hospital. She had gall bladder disease. Pretty common for a woman at her age and stage.

Medical coding was complicated. There were so many long strings of numbers, and changes and revisions happened all the time. All it would take was for someone to transpose a couple of numbers for things to go awry. Usually, it was just a matter of straightening out the codes so the insurance companies paid up. It definitely led to angry patients, but usually not so angry that they'd kill someone. Threaten to sue? Sure. Murder? Morgan didn't think so.

In this case, though, the incorrect coding caused Mary Pickett to be referred to hospice care for Stage IV pancreatic cancer. Her doctor had called her and informed her of the diagnosis and scheduled a follow-up appointment. She'd done some Internet research and decided that she didn't want to go through the pain and misery of waiting out a terminal diagnosis.

She'd made a big dinner for her family, cooking all of their favorite dishes, and the next morning she'd shot herself in the head.

Her son had sued, but while everyone was saddened by what had happened to Mary, no one thought the hospital's mistake rose to the level of requiring any compensation to her family or any punishment for the doctor who hadn't looked closely enough at the test results or for the clerk who had transposed the numbers.

Mary Pickett's family had gotten nothing. Not even an apology from the hospital.

Morgan shook his head. It was tragic and he didn't blame the family for being angry. He personally would be incandescent with rage. It still, however, made no sense for this case. Mary Pickett hadn't been one of his patients. Lexa wouldn't have worked on her case while she was working with Morgan. She hadn't come in through the Emergency Department where Lexa had been before her rotation with his department, either. He couldn't figure out where they would have ever crossed paths, much less to the point where her family would somehow blame her for what had happened.

He drummed his fingers on his desk. Mary hadn't been his patient. That didn't mean he couldn't access her patient file. It just meant that he shouldn't. Ashley would have his head. He'd promised her that he wouldn't do this. Specifically. Although if it came to light, Ashley would be the least of his problems. She'd made it clear that she wouldn't run interference for him again. This would be on his head.

Which was already heavy with the guilt he felt over Lexa.

He put in his password and pulled up Mary Pickett's file. He was right. She'd never been Lexa's patient. He scanned page after page of the file. He found Michelle Schultz on page 4. She'd been the tech who ran the blood tests that confirmed the high amount of bilirubin in

Mary's bloodstream. Brianna Olson turned up on page 9. She'd been the nurse who had helped Mary when she got her CT Scan.

He didn't find Lexa's name until page 14 of the file. A chill ran through him. He remembered this now. Lexa had covered an overnight shift for another one of the residents. The only reason she was in this file was that she'd signed off on some bloodwork that had been run. She'd probably never even seen the results. Mary hadn't been her patient, but Lexa's name was there in the file.

There were other names in the file, too, though. People who, like Lexa, might not even know that they were in the sights of a killer. Any one of them might be in danger at this very moment.

Morgan hit a few buttons to forward the file to his personal email, shut down his computer, and ran, dialing Danielle's phone number as he went.

CHAPTER TWENTY EIGHT

Danielle's phone rang four times. Morgan could imagine her looking at the Caller ID and deciding whether or not to pick up. He offered up a prayer to the cell phone gods and apparently it worked.

"What is it, Morgan?" She did not sound happy to hear from him.

"I think I know how this whole thing started." He got to his car and unlocked the door. Getting in, he put Danielle on speakerphone.

"No, Morgan. I told you. You're too close to this. You're off the case."

"Please, Danielle!" He put the car in reverse and backed out of the spot, then headed for the exit. "Hear me out. I don't have to be part of anything, but you need to know about this."

There was a pause. "You're sure I need to?" Her tone was dry and she emphasized the word *need.*

"I am. It's too deep in the medical weeds. Please. I'm begging you. Hear me out. This killer is not done. There are several more targets. He could be out there now targeting one of them."

She sighed. "Meet me at the office, then. I'm still here."

Of course she was. She was every bit as obsessed with this case as he was.

Morgan careened through the streets, trying to make time but not cause an accident. His anxiety cranked up with every stoplight he hit. If this was the killer, who would he go after next? So far, his targets had all been small potatoes, medically speaking. A nurse. A tech. A resident.

They'd have to comb through the file to find any and all names. Who knew what logic the killer was using to decide who to grab, and when.

He left his car in a garage two blocks from the FBI building and ran. Good thing he'd been trying to live a little healthier. He didn't feel quite as out of breath as he had chasing down Connor.

He texted Danielle as he got to the FBI building. In a matter of minutes, she was opening the door for him and shepherding him through darkened quiet lobby. The lights had been dimmed and everything was in shadow. Their footsteps echoed on the hard surface of the floor. Without the bustle of people coming through, they sounded like gunshots.

"Start explaining," Danielle said as she hit the buttons for the elevator.

"A woman named Mary Pickett was mistakenly given a terminal diagnosis. She was told she had pancreatic cancer and had only three months to live."

Danielle winced. "Nasty stuff. My uncle died from it. It was fast and terrible."

The elevator came and they got in the car and Morgan continued his explanation. "The problem was that Mary didn't have pancreatic cancer. She had plain old ordinary gall bladder disease. Unpleasant, but completely curable."

"That sounds like that would have been good news." The doors pinged open and, once again, Danielle walked Morgan down to the conference room where the files on the case were still laid out.

He'd known it. She was as deep in this as he was. "Except Mary never heard that news. She did a little Internet research and decided to take her own life rather than spend her last three months in pain. She didn't want to go through it and she didn't want to put her family through it."

"Family?" Danielle asked. "What do we know about the family?"

"Besides her son being angry enough to try to sue the hospital? Not much." Morgan sat down at the conference table.

Danielle sat down across from him. "I take it the lawsuit didn't get him what he wanted."

"A judge threw it out almost instantly, even said that it was frivolous." Judge Lourdes Alvarez had made it abundantly clear that Mary's family didn't stand a snowball's chance in hell of getting any kind of settlement from the hospital and should, in fact, feel lucky that she wasn't going to make them pay the hospital's legal fees.

"That must have gone over well." Danielle had picked up a pen and was tapping it against the yellow legal tablet in front of her

"Not exactly. Apparently, a few threats were made by the son. He had to be removed by the bailiff. The judge opted not to hold him in contempt, and said she understood that the man was in pain."

"All right. Give me the names again," Danielle said, pulling her laptop in front of herself.

"Mary Pickett. Her son is Tyler."

Morgan paced the room while Danielle ran the names through some law enforcement databases. She made a strange noise in the back of her throat.

"What?"

"Tyler Pickett was issued a ticket for loitering near one of the hospital's entrances around a week ago. He didn't cause any trouble so no one made a special note of it." She typed some more. "Since his mother's death, he's quit his job teaching job at Buchanan High."

Had he quit his job so he could apply himself to seeking revenge full time? "What now?"

Danielle shut her laptop with a decisive snap. "Now we go talk to Tyler Pickett."

***

Danielle parked down the street from Pickett's house. Morgan got out of the car, ready to accompany her down the street, but she stopped him. "I think you should wait here."

The wind whipped up, making the treetops on the suburban street dance over their heads. Morgan shook his head. "No way. I'm not letting you confront someone who may have already killed three women alone."

She rubbed at the spot on her forehead between her eyebrows with her thumb. "You do know that I'm an FBI agent, right? And you're not?"

Morgan looked down at his feet. He was aware and also had seen her subdue two men, both bigger than her, while barely breaking a sweat. "I know. Please don't make me wait here. I swear I won't do anything to jeopardize the case."

"Or your own safety?" She glared at him. "Because that happens to be important to me as well."

"Yeah. I know. You don't want to have to fill out the paperwork," he said, remembering her little joke.

She didn't laugh this time. "Yeah. It's more than that, though." She turned to face him. "Seriously, Morgan. I don't want you to get hurt."

He felt a flush start up his neck. "I get it," was all he could say, though.

Danielle blew out a breath. "Come on then."

Pickett's house was dark. There was no car in the driveway. Danielle rang the bell anyway. No answer and no movement within.

She pounded on the door, hard. "Tyler Pickett! Open up! This is the FBI. We need to talk to you."

Still nothing.

"You looking for Tyler?" A voice came from next door over the fence next to the driveway.

Danielle turned and walked over to an older white man wearing a Washington Nationals sweatshirt who was rolling trash bins to the curb. "We are. Have you seen him?"

"Sure did. Left about thirty minutes ago." The man set the garbage bin upright and scratched at the back of his neck. "In a bit of a hurry, too. Didn't want to stop to chat or anything."

"Does he usually chat?" Danielle asked.

The man grimaced. "Used to. Not since his mama died, though. He's having a hard time with that. Do you want to leave a card or something? I could let him know you were here and want to talk to him."

Danielle shook her head. "No thanks. Did he happen to say where he was going?"

The man shook his head. "No. Just waved me off. Said he had something urgent and would talk to me later."

Danielle and Morgan returned to the car. She stayed calm and cool until they got inside. Then she pounded her fist on the steering wheel. "Damn it. He could be out right now, tracking his next victim." She turned to Morgan. "Based on what you've seen so far, who do you think the next victim will be?"

It wasn't like Morgan hadn't been thinking about it. "I'm not sure. I don't think I quite understand the order he's going in unless it's just who he thinks he can get to when."

Danielle took a couple of deep breaths and then asked, "That could be. Who's left?"

"There's the clerk who made the actual billing error, but her name isn't in the file. Two techs from the imaging department. He hasn't hit the doctor who probably should have caught the error before he made that call." Morgan ticked each person on one of his fingers.

Twisting in her seat to look at Morgan, Danielle said, "If he's watching the news at all, he's got to realize we're getting closer to figuring out what the connection is between his victims. He might switch how he prioritizes because of that. Who do you think his primary target would be?"

“The doctor,” Morgan said with no hesitation. It was the way it worked. The doctor took the most responsibility always. They were where the buck stopped and there was no doubt in Morgan’s mind that this doctor had screwed it up.

“I agree. Do you know who the doctor is?” Danielle started the car’s engine.

“Dr. Clark.”

“You know him?”

Morgan stuck out his hand in a half-gesture. “We’ve met.”

“Can you call him?”

Doctors pretty much never have listed phone numbers. Their lives would be hell if they did. “It’ll take a minute to get the number.”

“Better get started now then.” Danielle pulled away from the curb.

Morgan called the hospital. “This is Dr. Morgan Stark. I need to get an urgent message to Dr. George Clark in Internal Medicine.”

“Just a moment, Dr. Stark. I’ll try his service.”

Meanwhile, Danielle was on her phone as well. “Hey, Gunther. It’s Danielle. I need an address for a Dr. George Clark. He works at Georgetown University. He’s in the Internal Medicine department.”

She listened for a moment. “Yeah. I’m concerned he might be our unsub’s next victim.”

Then the hospital operator was back on. “I’m sorry, Dr. Stark. Dr. Clark isn’t answering. Is he on call? Can I get someone else from his department for you?”

“No. Thanks.” He hung up and turned to Danielle. “No answer.”

“I’ve got an address. Let’s go.”

CHAPTER TWENTY NINE

Tyler Pickett sat in the back of his darkened van, watching people come and go. It was a quiet street. Suburban. Well-to-do. There wasn't much traffic. He was waiting for one person in particular. The person most responsible for the death of his mother.

His mother. The person who had believed in him, who had supported him, who had done everything for him. The kindest person he knew.

Dead. Because this asshole didn't know how to read a test result and let his decisions for his medical patients be decided by billing codes. Greedy.

As if the thoughts had summoned him, Dr. George Clark pulled his car into the driveway. Pickett jumped out of his car and trotted the few feet to the edge of the doctor's property. There he slowed his steps to a stroll. From the corner of his eye, he tracked the doctor's progress as the man parked his car in the detached garage.

As the doctor emerged from the garage, Tyler stopped on the sidewalk grabbed at his chest, took a few staggering steps, and collapsed.

"Hey! Are you okay?"

Tyler twitched a little, but didn't respond. He kept his face impassive as he listened for the doctor's approaching footsteps.

A hand shook his shoulder. "Hey! Buddy! What's going on? Can you talk?"

As he had with Michelle and Lexa and Brianna, Tyler grabbed the doctor's wrist with one hand while drawing his knife out with the other and slashing out with it.

It didn't go as smoothly this time.

He hadn't factored in how much bigger and stronger Clark was than the three women he'd already killed. The doctor wrenched away, springing to his feet. "What the hell?" He grabbed his arm where a line of red was already soaking through his white shirt and sprinted for his front door.

Tyler got to his feet nearly as quickly as Clark, but the doctor had a head start on him. Clark made it to the front door and punched in a code on a keypad next to the door. The door popped open and Clark was almost through it when Tyler caught up to him. Launching himself forward, he knocked Clark the rest of the way into the house, landing on top of him.

This was better than what he'd planned. He could take his time now without worry that a passerby would see them.

As Tyler turned, Clark twisted beneath him so they were facing each other. "Who are you? What do you want?" His chest heaved as he panted with the exertion.

"Take a good look, doc. Can you guess who I am?"

Clark searched his face. "No. No. I've never seen you before. Who are you?"

Typical. This man had wreaked devastation on Tyler's world and didn't even recognize him. The arrogance of these doctors! "My name is Tyler Pickett. My mother was Mary Pickett. Ring any bells?"

Clark stopped struggling beneath him. "No. It doesn't ring any bells. Should it?"

"Let me refresh your memory, doc." Tyler shifted so he had the doctor pinned beneath his knees. "You told my mother she had three months left to live. You told her that her final days would be full of pain and misery and that there was absolutely no hope for anything else."

Clark recoiled. "No! No! You've got the wrong guy. I swear! It's not the kind of diagnosis I give! I'm a pediatrician, for God's sake! I don't treat adults. Only kids! Even if I did, I would never have presented anything to a patient in that way!" He struggled against Tyler.

"Well, you did. And what's even funnier about it, doc. Bear with me, this is a good one. You were wrong. Some clerk in the billing office inverted some numbers and you never even bothered to check the actual test results. If you had, you would have found out that my mother had years in front of her. Happy, healthy years."

Clark shook his head violently. "I'm telling you that you have the wrong doctor! I treat children. You have the wrong guy. I'm begging you! Please! Listen to me. I am not the person you're looking for."

"Is that how you sleep at night? By telling yourself that? Just erasing it from your memory?" Tyler held the knife to the edge of Clark's jaw. "Because I can't sleep at night. You know why? Because once my mother heard what the next miserable months of her life were going to be like, she killed herself. She didn't want to put herself or me or the rest of our family through such a hopeless and horrible end."

"What?" Clark's eyes flew open wide. "That's terrible! I would definitely remember that. If that happened, it wasn't me who did it! It's not me!"

"Oh, it was you, all right. And I'm here to make sure that you never do that to another family, that you never wreak that kind of destruction and grief anywhere ever again."

Tyler lifted his knife high. "How about I remind you of exactly who my mother was?"

"No!" Clark shouted.

CHAPTER THIRTY

Morgan followed Danielle to the front door of George Clark's house. She banged on the door three times with her first which Morgan had come to recognize was a bit of a ritual for her. "FBI!"

He strained to listen. Could Pickett have gotten here first? Was he already inside? Were they too late?

Inside, there was a scuffling noise and then a shout. Danielle's eyes narrowed and her head cocked a bit to one side. She knocked again. "Dr. George Clark! This is the FBI! Please open the door!"

There was a thump as if something had been knocked over. Morgan's heart raced. He looked over at Danielle.

"Dr. Clark!" Danielle knocked again, then reached down to try the knob.

The door was unlocked.

"I'm going in," she told Morgan. "Please, for the love of God, stay here."

Before he could answer, she'd unholstered her weapon and banged the door open. "FBI! Everybody freeze!"

"What the hell?" A man's voice yelled. "Is this some kind of joke?"

Danielle came back to the door a couple of seconds later and motioned for Morgan to come in with her. Her weapon was back in its holster.

Morgan followed her in to find George Clark on the living room floor where he'd clearly been wrestling with this two sons. A side chair had been knocked onto its side. That must have been the thump. Clark and his kids probably hadn't heard the knock on the door over the noise of their own roughhousing.

"I assure you, Dr. Clark. This is no joke," Danielle said.

Morgan stepped forward. "George. It's Morgan Stark here. From Georgetown. Can we ask you some questions?" He exchanged a look with Danielle. If Clark was Pickett's next target, it didn't seem like he was here. Had Morgan gotten it wrong again?

Clark got up from the floor. "Morgan! Good to see you. Absolutely. Hold on a second. Let me get these ruffians settled." He turned to the kids. "Do you guys want to watch some cartoons?"

Both the boys jumped up and down. "Yes! Cartoons!"

"Fine. Just don't tell Mom, okay?" Clark winked at Morgan. "I'll be right back." He left the room with the kids.

"Could we have beaten Pickett here?" Morgan asked Danielle.

Danielle blew out a breath. "I'm not sure. Something's not right, though."

Clark came back into the room and motioned for Danielle and Morgan to come in. "So what's this about?" he asked.

"Mary Pickett," Morgan said.

Clark's face fell. "We probably should sit down. That was a bad one." He turned to lead them into the living room. "Do you want a glass of water or something?"

Danielle shook her head. "I'm afraid we're in a bit of a hurry, Dr. Clark. What can you tell us about Mary Pickett?"

Clark scratched at his neck. "Probably the worst mistake I've made in my entire medical career." He turned to Morgan. "You know how it is when you come in on Monday morning and there's a stack of files and test results on your desk?"

Morgan nodded. He did know. The hospital ran 24/7/365. If doctors took a weekend off, they were likely to come back to a lot of paperwork that needed to be sorted through.

"I had a full slate of patients to see that day so I wanted to move my way through all of that as quickly as I could." Clark sat down at the huge central island and rubbed his hand over his face. "Most of the time, it's pretty straightforward. On that particular day, though . . ." His words trailed off.

"Please, Dr. Clark," Danielle said.

"Right. You're in a hurry. Although I can't see why. All of this happened months ago and it's not like there's anything to be done to change it. The lawsuit was dismissed, too. I never even had to come into court," Clark said. "Anyway, that morning I picked up a patient's file, saw the billing code that indicated a very specific diagnosis, a very bad, very specific diagnosis. I called the patient to give her the bad news. I scheduled an appointment with her for the next day so we could talk more about her options. We hung up."

"Did she come in for the appointment?" Morgan asked.

Clark shook his head. "No. She did not. Because she was already dead. She'd killed herself. It wasn't until several days later that I went back through her file and realized that it had been the wrong billing code. She didn't have pancreatic cancer. She had gall bladder disease. Unpleasant enough, but not fatal. By then it was too late."

"What was the reaction from her family?" Danielle asked.

"Not good, as you can imagine. The son tried to sue us, but you know how these cases are. There are standards that have to be met and while I felt terrible about what happened, my lawyers and the hospital lawyers were very clear that this did not rise to that level. They were surprised the son was able to get anyone to take his case on. It didn't go far, though. The first judge dismissed it out of hand."

That fit with what Morgan had found out. "Did the son try anything else? Did he threaten you physically?"

Clark's eyes opened. "I think things got heated at the actual hearing, but like I said, I wasn't there. If he threatened me specifically, I don't know about it. He might have posted some fairly nasty reviews on some of those rate-your-doctor sites."

"Did you try to get him to stop?" Danielle asked.

Clark shook his head. "No. I felt terrible about the role I'd played even if it didn't meet the malpractice standards. He had a right to be angry."

"Have you received any other threats recently? Seen anything out of the ordinary? Felt like you were being watched?" Danielle asked.

Clark shook his head again. "No. Why?" Realization dawned on his face. "Does this have to do with those three young women who were killed?"

"We think so," Danielle said. "But there's been nothing you've noticed? No one following you? Nothing like that?"

The doorbell rang. Clark stood up, but Danielle rose and stopped him. "Are you expecting anyone?"

He shook his head. "No. Not really."

The doorbell rang again. A shot of adrenaline flowed through Morgan. Was this it? Was it Pickett? He'd lured his other victims by pretending to need help. Maybe he was doing the same thing here, ringing the doorbell and maybe asking if he could use the phone? Or saying his car had broken down?

Danielle said, "Okay. I'm going to come with you to the door, but don't do anything until I give you the okay."

Clark stared at her for a second. "You really think I'm in danger?"

"I know you are." Danielle drew her weapon, but kept it down by her side. "Morgan, step over there so you're out of the line of sight from the doorway."

He started to argue, but the look on Danielle's face made it clear that she wasn't going to back down. Morgan stepped aside, poised to help, but determined to show Danielle that he could control himself. He would not be thrown off this investigation again. He could and would help solve this case.

Danielle whispered to Clark who called out. "Who is it?"

"It's Henry from down the street, George."

Danielle looked over at Clark who nodded. She stepped back, but kept her weapon drawn. "Go ahead and open it," she said quietly.

Clark stepped forward and opened the door.

A man said, "Hey, George. Got a few letters for you. Post office can't seem to handle more than one person on a block named Clark." The man handed a few envelopes to Clark.

"Thanks. Such a bother."

"Yeah. Second time this week. You'd think they'd figure it out."

"Thanks." Clark shut the door. "Neighbor down the street," he said to Danielle. "We have the same last name and the post office is constantly delivering our mail to each other. Curse of a common last name, I guess."

A common last name. A pretty common first name, too. Maybe there was a different kind of mishap happening here. Clark had said he hadn't been in court when the son was there. Maybe he didn't know what he looked like. Maybe he didn't know to check what department the doctor worked in. Maybe he found one Dr. George Clark and didn't bother to look any further. Morgan pulled out his phone and hit the button to call Ashley.

"Is everything okay, Morgan?" That honeyed voice held a note of concern for him that made his heart leap a little and then clench. Once she found out that he'd broken yet another promise to her, she'd be through with him. There was no time for that now, though. If Morgan was right, another doctor was in danger.

"Yes. Of course," he lied. "I'm just double-checking something I saw in the roster. Does Georgetown have two doctors named George Clark?"

Ashley snorted. "We do. It's terribly confusing for everyone. One's in Internal Medicine and the other is in Pediatrics. Why?"

"Just trying to sort out something. I'll call you back later and explain." He hung up, feeling sick to his stomach. Had he gotten it right and still not been able to save someone? He ran over to Danielle.

“There are two Dr. Clarks at Georgetown. We’ve got the right one, but what if Pickett doesn’t?”

***

This time, Danielle didn’t bother parking down the block. She pulled right into Dr. Clark’s driveway, right behind his open garage door. A messenger bag lay on the grass of the front lawn.

Danielle ran to the front door with Morgan right on her heels. It was ajar.

“No! I’m telling you! You’ve got the wrong doctor!” A voice cried from within.

Danielle banged the door open, entering with her weapon drawn. “FBI! Freeze!”

Tyler Pickett had the other Dr. George Clark pinned to the floor. There was a knife in his right hand that he held high over his head. Pickett looked over his shoulder at Danielle and shifted to put Clark between him and the agent, using him as a human shield. “Stay back!” Tyler yelled.

There was no way for Danielle to shoot Pickett without potentially hitting Clark. “Let him go, Pickett. You can’t win this,” Danielle said, taking a small step forward. “Let him go.”

Morgan crept in, careful to stay out of the line of fire. He’d dealt with plenty of distraught people during his years in medicine. He called on all that experience now. “Listen to me, Tyler. You’re making a mistake here. We know why you’re doing this and this is not the Dr. George Clark that made that mistake.”

“So he keeps saying.” Tyler stood, hauling Clark with him. The doctor cried out in pain.

Morgan looked over at Danielle who gave him a small head nod. He stepped a little further into the room. “He’s telling the truth, Tyler. It wasn’t him. There are two doctors named George Clark at Georgetown. This isn’t the right one. This guy’s a pediatrician. He treats kids. There’s no way he had anything to do with your mom. Let him go, Tyler. He had nothing to do with your mother’s death.” Morgan kept his voice low and even.

“You’re lying.” Pickett shook his head back and forth like a horse trying to shoo off flies.

“I’m not. I swear.” Morgan crept a little closer, still very aware of Danielle’s sight lines. “Agent Hernandez and I just came from the house of the doctor who gave your mother the false diagnosis. He freely admits it, says it was the worst mistake he's ever made."

The knife lowered a little. Tyler's hand shook. Sweat poured down his face.

Morgan swallowed hard. "That doctor made a mistake. He didn't double-check all the paperwork and he told your mother that she was going to die. Don't you see the irony here, though, Tyler? You didn't check carefully and you're about to take revenge on someone who had nothing to do with your mother's case. Nothing."

Tyler wavered, looking back and forth between Clark and Morgan. "No. I don't believe you."

"It's true. You've already done that, in fact. You've already taken the life of someone else who had nothing to do with your mother's case. Lexa Windham. She didn't treat your mother." Morgan's voice cracked.

Tyler's head shot up. "Her name was in the file! I saw it!"

"She signed off on some blood work while one of her fellow residents was out. Your mother wasn't her patient. She never treated your mother. She never met your mother. She made no mistakes. But you did. Now she's dead. How do you think her family feels, Tyler?" Morgan asked, trying to make his tone conversational when the words he spoke made him want to punch this man in the face. "How is what you're doing here any different than what that other doctor did? You're making mistake after mistake and people are dying because of it."

"Shut up shut up shut up!" Tyler shoved Dr. Clark away and lunged instead at Morgan. Morgan grabbed the arm that controlled the knife and wrenched it to the side. Both men fell to the floor in a twisting, writhing heap.

Morgan's knee and elbow hit the ground hard. Pain radiated through him. The knife slashed toward him again. He managed to twist away from it just in time, but how many more times would he be able to do that? "Take the shot, Danielle!"

"I can't," she yelled. "Not without hitting you."

For a moment, everything seemed to slow down to Morgan. It was as if he could see Tyler moving in slow motion while his own mind raced. He knew anatomy. He knew where people's weaknesses were. The knife rose. He wasn't going to be able to avoid it again. If he could incapacitate Tyler, even for just a moment, he could get out of his grasp and out of Danielle's line of fire. The quickest way to do that would be to interrupt the blood flow to his brain by constricting the carotid artery. Morgan turned his hand and with the side of it, hit Tyler as hard as he could in the neck, just below his jaw.

Tyler slumped for only a second, but it was long enough for Morgan to scramble out of Danielle's way and put Tyler directly in her sights. "Take the shot, Danielle! Take the shot!"

A bang rang out and Tyler screamed and then twisted away from Morgan grabbing his leg. Danielle had her cell phone out before Morgan could even register what was happening. "This is FBI Special Agent Danielle Hernandez. Badge Number 5551234. I need emergency services and police back-up at 2734 Tulip Road."

Morgan's chest heaved with the effort he'd made. Panting, he looked over at where Tyler grabbed at his leg. Danielle had clearly been shooting to wound rather than to kill. There was too much blood, though. Way too much. It was pumping out onto the floor with every breath Tyler Plunkett took.

"How far out is the ambulance?" Morgan called to her.

"They're saying four minutes," Danielle replied as she checked over Dr. Clark for injuries.

Pickett might have four minutes, but Morgan doubted it. At the rate he was bleeding, he'd be past saving by the time the EMTs arrived to treat him. To survive, someone needed to apply a tourniquet to the leg, shut down the bleeding.

Morgan knew exactly what to do and how to do it, but how far was Morgan willing to go to save the man who had blown a whole in his heart by murdering Lexa? What about Michelle's family? Brianna's? The three women had been doing their jobs. They'd done nothing wrong, but they were all dead because of this man. Morgan could stop the bleeding, keep the man alive until the ambulance arrived.

But should he?

Lexa would have made such a fine doctor. Not only would she not have a chance to fulfill that dream, but how many patients would suffer because they wouldn't get the kind of care that she would have provided? This man had been trying to take out people who had made a mistake and had probably condemned countless others to seeing doctors that weren't nearly as good or as compassionate as Lexa Windham.

There it was. Lexa's compassion. Her empathy. It was one of the things that had made her such an exceptional doctor. What would she have thought of Morgan if there was one life that could have been saved and he did nothing to do it?

He took off his shirt, ripped off the sleeve and began wrapping it tightly around Tyler Pickett's leg. The flow of blood from his gunshot wound slowed. Morgan used the other part of his shirt to staunch what was left, gratified to see it take a little longer for the blood to soak through.

Danielle crouched down next to him. "Is he going to be okay?"

Morgan nodded. "For what it's worth, yeah."

The sound of sirens split the night. Help was almost there.

CHAPTER THIRTY ONE

"Come on, doc," Danielle said. "I'll give you a ride home. I think we've done all we can here."

Morgan looked into the emergency room bay. Tyler Pickett lay handcuffed to a gurney. He'd need surgery, but he'd live. He'd have to pay for the destruction that he caused eventually, but Danielle was right. At the moment, there was nothing more for Morgan here. He looked around the bustling department. There'd been a time when all he'd needed was the energy of this place or one like it. The assemblage of symptoms and test results would dance in his head until they coalesced into a diagnosis, which he could then deliver. It had made everything he did seem worthwhile.

Not anymore. Now it all seemed empty. He knew it had started before Lexa's murder, but that had sealed it all. He didn't belong here anymore.

"Thanks," he said to Danielle. "A ride home would be great."

They'd been at the hospital getting checked over and answering questions all night. He was exhausted. They walked out into the pale spring sunlight of a new day.

"You don't look happy," Danielle said. "We caught the bad guy. It's over."

Morgan blew out a breath. "It is definitely over."

Danielle squinted at him. "You miss her, don't you? Lexa was more than just another resident to you, wasn't she?"

He nodded, not quite trusting himself to speak. "Working with her was changing things for me. I was starting to rediscover the joy of my job. Now . . . now, I don't know how I'll ever get that back." He kicked at the sidewalk. "I'm not sure I want to."

She stopped on the sidewalk. "Her death really shook you."

It wasn't a question, but Morgan answered anyway. "More than I can describe."

She frowned and rubbed her forehead. "I should have realized. It's not like I haven't been there myself."

Morgan looked up at her in surprise. "You? You seem like you're always so focused."

"Yep. That's me." She laughed, but it didn't sound like she thought anything was funny. "A little too focused. Otherwise I might have seen what getting you involved in this case was doing to you. I would never have dragged you into all this if I'd realized what the impact would be. I'm sorry."

"Don't be." Morgan put a hand on her arm. "I'm not sure what I would have done if I hadn't been able to help you. I was headed to a pretty dark place already. Knowing that I could still have some positive impact was huge for me."

"It's pretty much what keeps me going, too." She slipped on her sunglasses. "Maybe we should do it again someday."

***

Morgan had just tied on his running shoes when the buzzer for the front door rang. Strange. He wasn't expecting anyone. The only person who had been by in ages was Danielle and he was fairly certain she'd be busy writing reports about now. He hit the intercom button. "Hello?"

"Morgan. It's Ashley. Can I come up?"

He smashed the button to unlock the door so fast he hurt his finger. What was Ashley doing here? His heart did that little leap it always seemed to do at the sound of her voice. Could she maybe be coming to talk about them reconciling? Probably shouldn't get his hopes up. Instead, he did a quick survey of the apartment. It wasn't going to get a spread in *Home & Garden*, but it wasn't a pit.

It felt like forever, but eventually Ashley knocked on the door.

He opened it and let her in. "To what do I owe the pleasure?"

She grimaced. "It's not going to be much of a pleasure for either of us."

Uh oh. Not a reconciliation then. He gestured to the couch with his head. "Do you want to sit down?"

"I think that would be best."

"Coffee? Glass of water?"

She shook her head. "It's not a social call, Morgan."

He'd gathered that. "So what is it?"

She sat down on the couch and crossed her legs at the ankle. Always the lady. "There's going to be a hearing regarding your recent actions."

He frowned. "Which ones?"

"There's more than what we talked about before?" Her eyebrows went up, then she held up her hand to stop him from answering. "I don't want to know any more than I already know, Morgan. I was able to run some interference when you first started going through patient files and using that information to help the FBI. I only had one Get Out of Jail Free card for you, though. The fact that you continued to do that even after I warned you . . ." She sighed and shook her head. "Long story short, there's going to be a hearing."

Okay. He understood that. At least, they'd hear his side. "What kind of hearing?"

"One that will decide your future with the hospital and possibly your future in medicine." She leaned forward, long blonde hair falling over her shoulder. "Morgan, you could lose your license."

He reared back. "No. That's . . . that's too extreme."

She shrugged. "Maybe. It's the worst-case scenario, for sure, but it's still a possibility."

Okay. Things didn't always end up at the worst-case level. "What's the best case?"

"The hospital suspends you for a period of time without pay."

Morgan leaned back in his recliner chair. Ashley had warned him. She'd done her best to cover for him. "I guess we'll cross whatever bridge they throw up when we get to it."

She gazed at him, confusion plain on her face. "I didn't expect you to take this so calmly. Medicine has been your life for so long. I thought you'd be devastated."

Oddly, he wasn't. He tried to figure out why. "A week or two ago, I might have been. Although I think that would have been disingenuous." He leaned in now, too. Trying to put his feelings into words. "I loved medicine. I loved becoming a doctor."

She smiled. "I remember. I was there. You'd come home every night jazzed up and excited about what you'd learned and who you'd helped."

"When was the last time you saw me like that?" He remembered those days, too. They'd been amazing. He'd loved what he did.

She shook her head. "I'm not sure."

"Exactly." When was the last time? He'd felt a glimmer of it working with Lexa, when they'd stopped Ayres from operating on Vincenzo Rohr. But before that? He didn't remember. It had been weeks. Maybe months. Could it have been years? "Look. I screwed up.

I knew what I was doing. I felt the risks were worth the reward so I did it."

"And were they? Were the risks worth the reward?" Ashley asked.

He'd caught a killer. Just thinking the words to himself made his heart soar. He'd used everything he had—his intellect, his powers of observation, his body—and he'd help bring about a small modicum of justice in the world. "Yeah. Totally worth it. No matter what happens next."

That was the big question, wasn't it? What would happen next? To figure that out, he'd need to come to terms with some of the things in the past. It was too late for it to fix anything, but he needed to say it. "Ashley?"

"Yes, Morgan."

"I'm sorry."

She waved his words away. "You don't need to apologize. I'll be fine. No one's blaming me for what you did."

"I don't mean that," he said. He looked down at his hands that he'd twisted together in his lap. "I'm sorry that I wasn't a better husband. You were always there for me and I was always there for my patients."

"Oh, Morgan." Her voice wobbled like she might be about to cry. "You're a good man."

"But I wasn't a great partner. I look back now at all the things you did that made my life better and how little I appreciated the kind of person you are." It might be too late now, but he needed to say it to her. He needed her to understand that he got it, finally. "I'm sorry and I want you to know that I'm going to try to do better."

"Thank you," she said, her voice small. She sniffed and then blew out a breath, regaining her composure. "What will you do if they take away your license, Morgan?"

A weight lifted off his shoulders. "They can take my license, but they can't take away what I know. I can find ways to put that to good use." He could think of dozens of ways to do that, but there was one that stood out. What was it that Danielle had said? That they should do that again someday?

Maybe someday would come sooner than expected.

Tomorrow, he'd call Danielle.

And find out just what he'd have to do to take on a permanent position with the FBI.

NOW AVAILABLE!

TOO CLOSE

(A Morgan Stark FBI Suspense Thriller—Book 2)

While Morgan Stark, a brilliant doctor, trains to become an FBI agent, he is needed urgently: a new serial killer is targeting young women, leaving medical clues that only Morgan can decipher. But with a diabolical killer on a spree, is Morgan in over his head?

"A brilliant book. I couldn't put it down and I never guessed who the murderer was!"
—Reader review for Only Murder

TOO CLOSE is book #2 in a new series by #1 bestselling and critically acclaimed mystery and suspense author Rylie Dark, which begins with TOO LATE (book #1).

Morgan Stark is a renowned surgeon, acclaimed by his colleagues for his brilliance as a diagnostician. But when his close friend and protégé resident is murdered, Morgan feels compelled to help the FBI decipher the trail of medical clues and bring the killer to justice.

FBI Special Agent Quinn Carter, 28, a rising star in the BAU, equally esteemed by her colleagues for her brilliance and determination, is not used to turning to a doctor for help in solving crimes. This unlikely partnership, though, may just surprise them both.

A string of women are found murdered, and Morgan feels certain that they share a similar medical history. But with medical records lost or sealed for privacy, will his assumptions lead him down the right road?

Or will he make a mistake, and fail to save the next victim in time?

A cat-and-mouse thriller with harrowing twists and turns and filled with heart-pounding suspense, the MORGAN STARK mystery series offers a fresh twist on the genre as it introduces two brilliant protagonists who will make you fall in love and keep you turning pages late into the night.

Book #3 in the series—TOO FAR GONE—is now also available.

"I loved this thriller, read it in one sitting. Lots of twists and turns and I didn't guess the
culprit at all… Already pre-ordered the second!"
—Reader review for Only Murder

"This book takes off with a bang… An excellent read, and I'm looking forward to the next book!"
—Reader review for SEE HER RUN

"Fantastic book! It was hard to put down. I can't wait to see what happens next!"
—Reader review for SEE HER RUN

"The twists and turns kept coming. Can't wait to read the next book!"
—Reader review for SEE HER RUN

"A must-read if you enjoy action-packed stories with good plots!"
—Reader review for SEE HER RUN

"I really like this author and this series starts with a bang. It will keep you turning the pages till the end of the book and wanting more."
—Reader review for SEE HER RUN

"I can't say enough about this author! How about 'out of this world'! This author is going to go far!"
—Reader review for ONLY MURDER

"I really enjoyed this book… The characters were alive, and the twists and turns were great. It will keep you reading till the end and leave you wanting more."
—Reader review for NO WAY OUT

"This is an author that I highly recommend. Her books will have you begging for more."

—Reader review for NO WAY OUT

Rylie Dark

Bestselling author Rylie Dark is author of the SADIE PRICE FBI SUSPENSE THRILLER series, comprising six books (and counting); the MIA NORTH FBI SUSPENSE THRILLER series, comprising six books (and counting); the CARLY SEE FBI SUSPENSE THRILLER, comprising six books (and counting); and the MORGAN STARK FBI SUSPENSE THRILLER, comprising three books (and counting).

An avid reader and lifelong fan of the mystery and thriller genres, Rylie loves to hear from you, so please feel free to visit www.ryliedark.com to learn more and stay in touch.

BOOKS BY RYLIE DARK

SADIE PRICE FBI SUSPENSE THRILLER
ONLY MURDER (Book #1)
ONLY RAGE (Book #2)
ONLY HIS (Book #3)
ONLY ONCE (Book #4)
ONLY SPITE (Book #5)
ONLY MADNESS (Book #6)

MIA NORTH FBI SUSPENSE THRILLER
SEE HER RUN (Book #1)
SEE HER HIDE (Book #2)
SEE HER SCREAM (Book #3)
SEE HER VANISH (Book #4)
SEE HER GONE (Book #5)
SEE HER DEAD (Book #6)

CARLY SEE FBI SUSPENSE THRILLER
NO WAY OUT (Book #1)
NO WAY BACK (Book #2)
NO WAY HOME (Book #3)
NO WAY LEFT (Book #4)
NO WAY UP (Book #5)
NO WAY TO DIE (Book #6)

MORGAN STARK FBI SUSPENSE THRILLER
TOO LATE (Book #1)
TOO CLOSE (Book #2)
TOO FAR GONE (Book #3)

www.ingramcontent.com/pod-product-compliance
Lightning Source LLC
Chambersburg PA
CBHW030614310726
48979CB00003B/709
9781094395098